SET
A Love Story
A NOVEL

Karen Dodson

PESCA
PUBLISHING

An imprint of Reveal Patagonia, LLC

Published by Pesca Publishing
A division of Reveal Patagonia, LLC
6248 Waterman Avenue, St. Louis, Missouri 63130

Live the adventure: revealpatagonia.com

COVER ART BY GEORG MICIU
COVER AND BOOK DESIGN BY MARCY MAMROTH
EDITED BY MARY ELLEN BENSON

Summary: Kate is a successful journalist at the *Chicago Tribune* who suffered trauma and loss as a child. One day, she reconnects with Andrew, an old friend. When he takes her on a fly-fishing trip to the beautiful and exotic region of Patagonia, Argentina, she falls in love with Nico, their kind and handsome Argentine fishing guide. When Kate is scheduled to leave, she faces a powerful dilemma: Should she risk everything to move to Patagonia for the possibility of a romance with Nico? Does Nico care for her as much as she cares for him? How does she tell Andrew, who is in love with her, yet can't express it because of his own difficult past?

ISBN 978-0-9862359-1-7

Digital editions (EPUB and MOBI formats) produced by Booknook.biz

For my husband Ed.
Thank you for teaching me how to fish. *Te amo.*

Nov 2015

For Kelsey,
Safe travels to
Patagonia - you'll fall
in love with it like
I did! All best,
Karen
Dodson

SET
A Love Story

PART I

CHAPTER 1
CONNECT

I love Chicago-style hot dogs, and that's what I'm holding when I run into Andrew, literally. It's noon on a frigid November Saturday and Chicago's sidewalks are packed with lunchtime shoppers. Shivering despite my wool coat and hat, I wait in line at my favorite hot dog cart on Michigan Avenue. The cart's distinctive red umbrella is flapping in the wind and I march in place to keep warm. Finally I'm served. After thanking Dominic, the vendor, I quickly turn and bump into the next person in line, a man wearing a thick black jacket, Cubs baseball cap and sunglasses. My sandwich, piled high with tomatoes and peppers, flies into the air, hits the man's arm and falls to the ground. Bright yellow mustard splatters everywhere.

"I'm so sorry!" I cry as I grab a handful of napkins from the cart and begin to clean up the mess.

"No problem!" shouts the man, brushing onion bits off his sleeve. "I was too close. I'll buy you another!"

He lowers his sunglasses and smiles at me. When I look up, I see that it's Andrew, an old friend.

"Hey, Kate, I thought it was you," he laughs. "Geez, let's try this again; you know, where we call each other for lunch."

I smile and with mock disdain, slap him gently on his soiled arm. A brilliant and flamboyant litigator, Andrew always had a way of making me laugh. As a young journalist, I covered his trials for my hometown newspaper, and, in return, he taught me the law. Soon we became friends. When the *Chicago Tribune* hired me as its features editor, I moved downtown and we lost touch.

I'm surprised at how happy I am to see him. After we clear the mess, he leads me to a nearby bus shelter and removes his sunglasses and cap. His hair, once a light blond, is turning gray. I notice that he hasn't shaved for a few days.

"Kate, you look great!" he shouts, pulling me into the shelter. "Let's go somewhere else for lunch, my treat."

I'm reluctant to say yes since I'm on deadline, and Gus, my impatient city editor, is waiting for me. I pause for a moment and watch a bus as it stops near our shelter with its brakes hissing loudly. When the driver opens its doors, nearly a dozen passengers dash down the steps and disperse onto the sidewalk. As the bus pulls away, the driver shuts its doors and I loosely cover my nose and mouth to guard against the exhaust.

I turn to Andrew and shake my head.

"I can't," I shout back. "I have to get to work. What are you doing here? Are you still in the suburbs?"

He leans close so that I can hear him.

"Nope," he replies, looking around. "I'm downtown now."

I grin, remembering the last time we were together. It was

three years earlier at the Thanksgiving Day Parade where we both arrived alone, yet stood only a few feet apart in the crowd. When we saw each other, we huddled to keep warm and waved at the floats. When the parade ended I told him I would call but didn't because I was married and so was he.

"How's Clay?" he asks. "Still with the Feds?"

"Yes," I nod, "but we broke up two years ago. How about you? Still with Annie?"

He looks down and pulls at his gloves. When he answers, his tone is bitter.

"She left me for another guy. Can you believe it? A teacher. They moved to D.C. I honestly don't care. They deserve each other."

I sense that he's hurting, so I gently lift his chin with my hand. When I let go, his stubble pulls a wisp of wool from my glove, and I remove it. I want to say something soothing, but a horn honks behind me.

"I'm sorry!" I shout. "You deserve better!"

My divorce had been amicable. Clay and I married immediately after high school and supported each other through college. After graduation, I worked days and nights as a beat reporter and Clay worked as a field agent for the FBI. He often traveled on assignment and we rarely saw each other. Soon we drifted apart. Though I knew the divorce made sense, I still felt lost and alone.

"I know!" Andrew replies, wiping his chin. "I do! Hey, I have an idea, want to go out? I mean, not out out, but just for dinner?

What do you think? That way, we won't have to shout at each other!"

I'm tempted to say yes, but I wonder if he's asking for a date. I don't see us as lovers.

"OK, how about lunch?" I offer instead, as we start to walk. "That way, we really won't be going out out."

"Deal," he replies, pulling a scrap of paper and pen from his pocket. "My place tomorrow. Here's the address. Twelve o'clock sharp."

ANDREW LIVES IN A SMALL APARTMENT near Lincoln Park. When I arrive and ring his doorbell, I feel ambivalent. My life at the *Tribune* is chaotic and full of deadlines and I barely have time to buy groceries, let alone commit to a relationship. When Andrew opens the door, I grin. He's wearing a stained green apron that says, "Beat the eggs, not the chef!" With a sweep of his hand, he invites me in.

"*¡Hola!*" he exclaims, closing the door. "Hungry?" I am. I smell curry and suddenly I'm glad I'm there. I walk through the doorway into his living room and set my purse on his couch. Nearby is a large mahogany desk and its surface is covered with piles of brightly colored feathers. Curious, I walk over and touch them.

"I tie flies," he explains, watching me. "For fishing."

My father was a fly-fisherman. A busy engineer, his favorite vacation was driving our family to Lake Michigan so he could fish from his old wooden drift boat. My mother hated going because she didn't fish and complained the entire time, especially on the drive to the lake. "Bob, for heaven's sake," she would say, "do you have to take four rods? There's no room for us!" He would just nod and smile.

When we finally arrived at the lake, he would rush to the dock to check on his boat. "Yep, she's ready!" he would say, always in his loudest voice. At daybreak he would row out onto the lake and we would see him in the distance casting his line.

Hours later he would come home, but without any fish. As he walked upstairs to change his clothes, my mother would say to me, the oldest, "I don't get it. He never catches anything, why does he bother?"

One summer my father rowed onto the lake but didn't come home. My mother called the Coast Guard and they found him dead on the bottom of his boat, still clutching his fishing rod. They told us it was a heart attack and that he was smiling.

During lunch Andrew tries to convince me that fishing is fun and hands me a fuzzy green object the size of a caterpillar.

"This is a fly," he explains as I roll it in my palm. "But the fish thinks it's a bug."

The fly has a hook and two plastic eyes.

"Dumb fish," I think, "this looks nothing like a bug."

"What happens when the fish realizes it's not food?" I ask out loud, trying to sound interested.

"That's the point," Andrew replies with a smile. "By the time you've set the hook it's too late. The fish will fight like mad to get off, but if you play it right you'll win. It's you against the fish, no mercy."

"No mercy," I repeat as I give him the fly, "sounds like fun." It's hard to hide my sarcasm.

"It *is* fun," he insists as he begins to clear the dishes. "You should try it. I'll teach you."

I stare at him and remember that my father died alone on Lake Michigan. I swallow hard, recalling how happy he was when he was fishing.

"OK," I say as I begin to load the dishwasher, "but just for a few hours and it isn't a date. It definitely isn't a date."

WEEKS PASS and we prepare for our fishing trip. Despite my busy schedule we find ways to spend more time together. He brings me dinner when I work late and I buy him an apron that says, "Fish with me, pleeease!" He buys me a rod and a reel and takes me to Grant Park to teach me how to cast so we can visit the Missouri Ozarks, warmer this time of year, to fish in its rivers.

"This is very expensive," he says, handing me the new reel one windy day as we stand next to Lake Michigan. "So whatever you do, don't drag it in the river. Also, when you hook the fish, don't bend the rod behind your head because it will break."

"Got it," I say with a mock salute. "I would never do that."

Then he introduces me to my fly, which is wrapped around a tiny hook. It's beautiful, with black and red feathers, orange rubber legs and strips of colored tinsel that sparkle in the sunlight. It's tied with a tiny knot to a nylon filament called a tippet, which is tied to a thicker filament called a leader. Both are tied to an even thicker nylon line, which is bright lime green.

Andrew demonstrates how to cast and though it looks easy, I soon learn that it's not. After my eighth try, he takes my rod and angles his arm backward, trying not to sound exasperated.

"Ten and two," he says slowly as he swings the rod behind him. "Imagine your hand is at two o'clock on a wall clock, that's when you stop the rod, like this." As he jerks the rod forward, he says, "Then you stop at ten o'clock. When you do it right, the rod will load itself."

The rod will load itself? Perfect, I think. This should be a piece of cake.

Our fishing destination is a small ranch in the Ozarks about a six-hour drive from Chicago. It's January, overcast and cold. The river, stocked with rainbow trout, flows inside the property and a lodge sits on a hill. We arrive midmorning, pick up our room keys and unpack the car. I walk along the riverbank, which has an abundant number of trees, and when I peer into the river I see a large school of trout. They're lined up like soldiers with their heads pointing upstream and their tails waving gently in the slow-moving water. Every few seconds an outlier swims slowly away.

Clearly, they feel safe, I think, as I glance at a sign that reads *Catch and Release.*

"How hard," I wonder, "can this be?"

Since Andrew wants to fish right away, I pull on my new wading pants. I want to wear my favorite Crocs, but Andrew bought me leather wading boots so I could walk safely on the river's rocky bottom.

"These will be a blessing," he explains, as I bend over to tie them up. I also have a new vest with myriad pockets that I packed with clippers, tippet, leader, extra sunglasses, a few flies, a bandana, sunscreen, ChapStick, and magnifying glasses. Because the pockets aren't marked, I figure it will take hours to find anything. Nevertheless, I snap on my wading belt, tuck my net inside and carefully step into the cold water. I feel ready to fish.

The first thing I catch is a tree. While casting backward I snag the fly in a low-lying branch and I struggle to yank it out. I pull gently on the rod, hoping to loosen the fly, but the fly snaps off along with the tippet. The leader and line, still tied together, fall like limp spaghetti to the water. I stare at the fly, wondering how long it will live in that tree, and hear Andrew as he wades over.

"No problem," he says cheerfully as he reaches into his vest. "I carry extra flies and tippet." I'm not surprised. Each of his pockets is bulging with miscellaneous objects and all, he claims, are essential. Tucking his rod under his arm, he snips off a piece of 4x tippet and ties it to the leader. Then he reaches into another pocket and pulls out a plastic container. Inside are dozens of colorful flies of various shapes and sizes. The smallest is the size of an ant. He removes a fly with a bright red body, maple-colored wings and a white tuft that indicates its head.

"This is a Royal Wulff," he explains as he knots it to my new tippet. "I tied it myself." He hands me my rod and as he wades away, squeezes my arm.

"Watch those trees," he warns, "and I'll be over here, just in case."

Two hours later, I'm ready to give up. Though my casting has improved, I haven't caught a fish. I'm hot and hungry and my fingers are cold. Suddenly, I feel a sharp pull on my line. I spin around searching for my fly, which has disappeared from the water's surface. Then a fish jumps in the distance and my reel comes alive, spinning and whining as the fish takes off.

"Fish! Fish!" I scream at Andrew. He looks at me and waves.

"Keep the rod tip high!" he yells. "Let him run!"

And run the fish does, zigzagging in the water and pulling the line, seemingly to get away. No mercy, I remember as I pull the rod tip up. Finally, after several minutes, I see the fish and it's smaller than it feels with a ruby-colored stripe that runs from its neck to its tail. I figure it must be tired by now and I drag it closer. To my surprise, it turns quickly and darts away before finally floating to the surface. Now what? I wonder. Remembering what Andrew taught me, I tuck the rod under my arm, grab my net and scoop the fish inside.

I look at the fish and it seems to look back, its gills flapping rapidly as it tries to breathe. It's beautiful, with gold, silver, copper, and ruby scales that glitter in the sun like precious gems. I want to examine it further, but since I also want it to live, I gently lower the net to the water and search for my forceps to remove the hook. Upper left pocket, I think, but the forceps aren't there. I pat my shirt and find them clipped to my collar. Andrew put them there to make them easy to find. As I unclip them, I wrap my hand around the fish's tail. Alarmed, it jumps out of the net and swims off, with my rod and very expensive reel trailing behind. I watch with dismay as the reel bounces along the rocks and hope that Andrew isn't watching. When I try to run to chase the rod handle, figuring I can grab it from the water, my sturdy boots feel like anvils. All I can do is wade.

I glance downstream and watch Andrew as he nets the fish and rescues my rod. He looks at me and smiles.

"Great job!" he shouts. "Isn't this fun?"

Still gripping the net, I give him a reluctant thumbs-up.

At dinner that night, we sit side by side and laugh about our day. After my first attempt, I caught several fish and Andrew is proud of me. Halfway through dessert, he carefully sets his fork on his plate and takes my hand.

"Nice work today, Kate," he says softly. "You're a good sport. I'm glad we ran into each other again." He wraps his arm around my shoulders and looks at me.

"How would you feel about going on a real date?" he asks. "That way we can see how things go before taking our relationship to the next level."

I look at him, surprised. Next level?

"Seriously?" I ask. "Is it because I caught so many fish today?"

"No, it's because I like you," he replies, laughing. "This isn't a proposal, Kate. It's just a date. No lifetime commitment. At least not yet."

Before responding, I take his hand, wondering if I could fall in love with him. Though handsome, strong and exceptionally smart, he rants and raves when he doesn't get his way and pouts for days. But like my father, Andrew is solid and dependable, and I can always count on him no matter what. "I always keep my promises," he would tell me. My father would say that, too. So despite my doubts – and because the wine that I'm drinking has weakened my judgment – I acquiesce.

"OK, let's give it a shot," I say, pulling his arm from my shoulders. "But I don't want you to think I like fishing or anything."

TWO MONTHS LATER, Andrew and I move in together, mostly because he wants to and I'm too busy at the *Tribune* to fight it. Dealing with daily deadlines is stressful, and I'm exhausted by the time I get home. When we begin to argue, I think it's relationship growing pains: who will cook and who won't, who will do the dishes and who won't, who will take out the trash and who won't. Andrew especially likes to educate me about loading the dishwasher. "The glasses go on *top*," he emphasizes, until I stop loading altogether out of spite. Soon I begin to feel micromanaged and controlled, and one night before dinner, I ask him about it.

"Chill out, Kate," he replies, pulling a roast chicken from the oven. "You get angry about nothing."

I frown and drop my handbag on the kitchen table.

"I never get angry about nothing!" I declare, tearing off a piece of chicken to eat. He gently slaps my hand.

"First of all," he scolds, "you shouldn't speak in double negatives. And second, don't eat with your fingers."

WEEKS GO BY and I spend more time at the office. Then one evening after dinner, Andrew hands me an envelope.

"Tickets to Patagonia, Argentina, m'lady," he says, with an exaggerated bow. "I fished there last year and we'll have guides. You'll love it."

"Argentina?" I ask. "Hmmm. Tango, Latin music, the new Pope? Sounds exotic." I'd heard that Patagonia was beautiful but never dreamed I'd get to visit. Our tickets say we're leaving in two weeks. I try to understand what this means.

"Andrew, first you forgive me when I drop a hot dog on your jacket. Then you teach me how to fly-fish. Then you invite me to live with you. Now you're escorting me to Patagonia. What gives? You really need a fishing buddy that badly?" He rolls his eyes.

"No, I have fishing buddies, but they aren't as pretty as you. Seriously, we'll have fun, plus the trout there are huge. Catching them will change your life."

CHAPTER 2

REVEAL

"Patagonia?" My best friend, Eva, sounds surprised. "Like the clothing company? Is it an actual place?" She is teaching me how to make cupcakes and I'm pulling ingredients from her refrigerator.

"Yes, Christopher Columbus," I tease, "it's a region in South America." I set three eggs on her granite countertop before continuing. "And P.S., we're going to the Argentina side of Patagonia. The other side is in Chile, next to the ocean. You know the ocean, that really, really deep body of water?"

Eva, who's scanning the recipe, stares at me over her reading glasses without smiling.

"And Gus let you take the time off on such short notice? Now *that's* a miracle."

The three eggs roll toward the sink, so I stop them with a dishtowel.

"Actually," I say, "he didn't let me take the time, I took the time. He wasn't pleased."

Eva walks over, sits on a barstool and runs her hand through her curly blonde hair.

"Katie," she says in her most serious voice, "a trip like this is a major commitment. Does Andrew know you're not happy?" She only calls me Katie when she wants to sound maternal.

"Yes," I respond. "He knows I'm not happy. He says it's my fault since I'm stressed because of work."

She scoffs and walks back to her post at the recipe book.

"Work, shmirk! Katie, he's always been like that! You hated working with him before and people don't change!"

I know she's right. Andrew could be mean and was known to throw tantrums in the courtroom. Once he was sanctioned by a judge and had to pay a large fine. "That judge is a moron," he told me when I asked him about it.

I pull a blue bowl from the cabinet and begin separating the eggs. I don't tell Eva what I'm thinking, which is I don't know if I love him.

"Anyway," I say, "I'm already packed. We spend one night in Buenos Aires then fly to a place called San Martín de los Andes that has lakes and rivers and the Andes Mountains. It sounds wonderful!" I pull a cupcake pan from the cabinet and set it on the counter.

Eva scans the recipe book with her finger and speaks to me at the same time.

"You know," she says slowly. "Andrew asked Jason if we wanted to go."

I look at her with disbelief. She doesn't know how to fish and is afraid of the water.

"Seriously?" I ask. "What did you say?"

She looks up from the book and makes a casting gesture. "I told him we're going!"

Eva and Jason rarely spend time apart. They grew up together in Lake Forest, Ill., attended Marquette University and got married after they graduated. Eva explained they were soul mates because, "We both like to sleep." After Clay and I broke up, Eva held me as I cried, wiped away my tears and told me to get over it. The loss was unbearable and I was paralyzed with grief. Eva, a devoted reader of pop psychology, thought I was simply reliving my father's death. She informed me that my mother, who couldn't deal with three children alone and drank too much, was likely an alcoholic. When I objected, she reminded me that I took care of my brother and sister and all of the household chores. She surmised that I was traumatized and not in touch with my feelings, which is why I spent so much time at work. Most of the time I ignored her, but sometimes wondered if this explained my divorce.

Now that Eva and Jason are going to Patagonia, I can't wait to leave. Gus, on the other hand, feels otherwise.

"Kate," he says, hovering at my desk one day at work, "you know this is the worst time to go anywhere. First of all, it's winter there and you'll be fishing in the snow."

I'm typing on my computer trying to ignore him, but stop and turn around. He's holding a cup of coffee, is at least 10 pounds overweight and I notice for the first time that he's balding.

"Gus," I say, amused, "it's autumn there. Did you take geography in school?"

Instead of laughing he mocks me in a loud voice.

"Did you take geography in school? No! I took an extra lunch!" Then he sits on the corner of my desk and lowers his voice. I know I'm about to be manipulated.

"Look, Kate, I'm serious. You know we're short staffed and I need you to cover Local, at least for a week. Please don't go."

I turn to my computer and type.

"Gus, I've worked every day for a month. I told you about this trip weeks ago. I'm going to Patagonia. Andrew is counting on me and you're just jealous."

He stands up and walks away, throwing his arms overhead.

"Yes, that's it! I'm jealous, *that's it*! And oh, by the way, there are no bathrooms in Patagonia where you're fishing, so you'll need to pee outside, and that I would love to see! Oh, and don't forget to send me the assessment papers before you leave. Joe's working on that. When things settle down in a few months, it's going on the front page. Trust me. Have a great time!"

When I don't respond, he stops and turns around.

"If you must go," he adds, "take notes about that country. The politics there are a mess."

THE MORNING WE LEAVE FOR PATAGONIA, Andrew hands

me a box wrapped in gold paper and tied with a red ribbon. I open it and reveal a brightly colored fly attached to a broach pin.

"I tied it myself," Andrew boasts.

"Thank you," I say as I give him a hug, "I love it!" I know that Andrew is trying to make up for his moody behavior, and at that moment I decide to forgive him.

"Truce?" he asks, hugging me.

"Truce," I answer, and kiss him on the cheek.

When we arrive at O'Hare Airport for our flight, we meet Eva and Jason in the American Airlines Admirals Club. They're sitting side by side on a brown leather love seat and jump up when we arrive. Andrew and I laugh when we see that they're wearing matching blue Patagonia shirts, olive-green fishing pants and brown Keen sandals. Eva also wears a cap with the words *Reel Diva* embroidered with red and yellow rhinestones on the front.

"*Voilà*!" she announces, slowly swiveling and making casting gestures, "I'm ready!" I grin and swivel back.

"Me, too!" I declare. "Did you practice your casting?"

Eva looks at me with a feigned painful expression.

"Yes, of course!" she squeals. Then she points to Jason, wrinkles her nose and adds, "He, however, did not."

Jason stands and adjusts his belt, then slaps Andrew on the back.

"Hey buddy," he says, "we'll have to step up our game since we're fishing with these ladies."

"Kate's already upped her game," Andrew replies, slapping

him back, "and you'll see that she's hard to beat."

We fly to the Dallas/Fort Worth International Airport to catch our 11-hour flight to Buenos Aires. In the air we watch movies and TV reruns on our seat monitors, and since I can't sleep, I ask our flight attendant to teach me a little Spanish. So far, I only know the word *gracias*, which probably won't get me very far.

"When you get there it will be morning," she instructs, "and you should say, '*Buenos días. ¿Cómo estás?*' That means 'Good morning. How are you?'" I repeat it slowly and wish I'd taken lessons before I left. I figure I can practice on Lola, our tour guide, who was referred by a friend and is going to greet us when we land.

When we descend into Argentina, we're served breakfast on tiny white trays.

"What's this?" asks Eva, who's sitting behind me. "It's supposed to be an omelet, but it looks like an enchilada and it's cold." I laugh, and since I'm not hungry, I give my omelet to Andrew. When we land at Ezeiza Airport, I'm excited and can't wait to see Argentina.

As we pull our bags from the overhead, Andrew instructs that we have to go through customs before we get to the terminal. I touch his arm, lean toward him and smile.

"I know," I admonish, "I'm not a moron."

As we ride the escalator down into the customs area, I look up and see a large sign with the word *Welcome* displayed in a dozen different languages. The sign hangs atop a wide glass partition and behind it is a large café of modern design, but no one is there. I decide it's empty because it's early. When we reach the first floor, we see two customs areas: one for international visitors and one for residents. The visitor area is full of travelers lined up serpentine style all the way back to the escalator.

"It will be at least an hour," chirps a young woman with long dark hair as she slings a giant Prada bag over her shoulder. She's heading to the line for residents.

"And another hour for baggage," she adds. "Good luck!"

Andrew drops his bag loudly on the floor.

"Seriously?" he yells. I feel his temper starting to rise. "Who but us travels at this time of day?" I feel myself get tense, waiting for his anger to explode.

Eva, rolling her eyes, pulls a cellophane bag from her purse, opens it and taps peanuts into my palm.

"Here," she says in a soothing tone, "since you didn't eat your omelet."

I pop them in my mouth.

"Thank you," I say as I chew. "I'm starving."

While we stand in line, I try to cheer Andrew up by suggesting we play "Guess where that person's from." We enjoy this game in Chicago when we go out for pizza since the city is a melting pot of ethnic groups. Eva and Jason join in, but Andrew is pouting and remains quiet.

"Mongolia!" whispers Eva, gesturing to a man in line. "Look at those fabulous eyes!"

Jason shakes his head. "Nope, China. And by the way, when have you ever been to Mongolia?" Eva slaps him on the arm.

"OK smarty," she says, pointing to a tall woman with blonde hair carrying a baby inside a sling that is held together with a large metal ring. "How about that woman?" Jason turns to look.

"Ah, definitely Sweden," he declares, "those Swedes are modern enough to have slings like that."

Andrew smiles.

"There you go," prompts Jason, "cheer up, we're on vacation and there's only two more hours before we see if our luggage made it."

When we finally enter the terminal, I feel overwhelmed by the crowd. Hundreds of travelers, most of them chattering in Spanish, are waiting, walking or running with luggage. I scan them looking for our tour guide. I hear her before I see her.

"Kate and Andrew, *¡Hoolllaaa!* Jason and Eva, over here!" I look ahead and watch the crowd part as a petite young woman pushes her way through. She's shorter than me, dressed in gaucho pants and a black tank top and large silver earrings swing from her ears. Her hair, which is brown, is casually knotted on top of her head and her smooth skin, dotted with perspiration, seems to shimmer. Her face is shaped like a heart and her dark brown eyes are huge.

"I'm Lola!" she cries as she hugs us. "Welcome to Argentina!" A young man approaches us pushing an empty luggage cart and takes our bags.

"That's Ramón," she explains. She directs him in Spanish while speaking to us in English, weaving it all into one long sentence.

"Welcome to Buenos Aires *lleva esos maletines alla, con cuidado!* (Take those suitcases there, be careful with them). How was your flight, do we have everything? *Protege tus dedos!* (Watch your toes). The van is this way, follow me!"

Lola's ebullient personality is energizing. We line up behind her like ducklings and try to keep up. She's clearly a force to be reckoned with, and I've already decided that I like her.

We're staying at the Alvear Palace Hotel, which is in the same neighborhood as La Recoleta Cemetery, where famous Argentines are buried. On the way, Lola stands near the passenger seat at the front of the van and, in delightful Spanish-tinged English, tells us about Buenos Aires, pointing out statues and buildings that mark its history. On one tall building there's a giant metal portrait of Eva Perón wearing a necklace and flower on her lapel. The portrait spans at least eight stories. Lola asks the driver to avoid the *villa miserias,* shantytowns, where thousands of residents live, and informs us that living conditions for most of the city's citizens are dire.

"Every day the peso is dropping in value," she explains. "This year, our inflation is nearly 30 percent."

Graffiti is everywhere – on buildings, fences and bridges – and when Jason asks, "Are they doing anything about it?" Lola answers, "No, it's a coveted art form."

"You're kidding!" Andrew chimes in, shocked.

"Graffiti artists are commissioned to paint buildings now," Lola continues as we pass a building with *¡Viva el Papa Francisco!* painted in colorful balloon letters on its facade. "Graffiti started in 2001 when the crisis against the government happened and people would start signing their names on the buildings. Now it's everywhere."

Soon we turn onto a street with bright pink, yellow, orange, green, and blue buildings and Lola explains that it's the La Boca neighborhood. I ask if we can walk around.

"No, let's just go to the hotel," Andrew moans, after he's been quiet most of the trip. I slump in my seat, but Lola tells the driver to pull over.

"We can, but just for a minute," she says. "We have time."

Eva, who is sitting next to me, nudges me in the ribs and leans over to whisper in my ear.

"I told you he was a jerk," she says.

By the time Lola drops us at our hotel, I'm exhausted and want to rest. She tells us to meet her in the lobby at 9 p.m. when she will take us to the "best steakhouse in Buenos Aires." In our room, I drop my purse on the floor and lunge to the bed for a nap. Andrew lies next to me and immediately starts snoring, so I pull the pillow over my head and try not to think of home. Gus has already sent me a dozen emails, and I'm determined not to answer them. Instead, drifting to sleep, I think of grass-fed beef and Malbec and hope that Andrew and I can get along.

At 8:45, I wake up and see Andrew pulling on his blazer. I leap out of bed and strip off my clothes.

"Hey," he admonishes, "we have 15 minutes until Lola gets here. You may want to get dressed." I run to the bathroom and close the door. The steam from Andrew's shower has covered the mirror and I wipe it with a towel. I splash cold water on my face and quickly brush my teeth as I turn on the faucet in the tub. The bathwater is too hot, but I climb in and begin to shampoo my hair.

"I'll meet you in the lobby!" yells Andrew, and I wonder why he didn't wake me sooner. Instead of worrying, I decide he meant well so I continue to rush to get dressed.

I get to the lobby at 9:15, and Lola's already waiting. She gestures to the van.

"Go ahead and get in!" she exclaims. Her tone is enthusiastic and energizing. "You can sit next to me!"

I'm wearing a strapless red dress and my wet hair clings to my back since there wasn't time for it to dry. I pull a black scrunchie from my purse and wrap my hair into a ponytail. As I click my seatbelt shut, Jason taps me gently on the shoulder.

"Did you get a nap, Kate?" he asks.

I turn to him gratefully.

"Yes," I answer, but Andrew interrupts.

"Where are we going, Lola?" he asks, holding onto his safety strap.

"Trust me," she responds with a grin. "The best steak in town, you'll see!"

We arrive at the restaurant at 9:30. I've decided that Lola can make anything happen and she proves that tonight.

"I hope you like it here," she says, leading us to a table by the window. "We're trying everything on the menu." The maître d' rushes over and she speaks to him in Spanish. Within minutes, four young male servers deliver several bottles of Malbec and large platters of food. There are cheeses and sausages, salads and breads – and those are just the appetizers.

"We'll have beef next," Lola adds, passing the platters like a nurturing mother, "then dessert. Now, please, my friends, go ahead and eat!"

Though I'm hungry, I decide to visit the ladies' room first. The restaurant pays homage to soccer, called *fútbol* here, and thus hundreds of soccer jerseys from all over the world are plastered on the walls and ceiling, some neatly framed inside hardwood molding. Even the barstools are soccer-oriented, with colorful balls tucked inside their bases. When I look down at the floor, I see that it's made of Plexiglas, designed so patrons can see the extensive wine cellar below. It feels funny to walk atop the bottles.

When I enter the ladies' room, I nearly bump into a woman who is helping a young girl wash her hands. Both of them look at me as I enter, and I smile. They are beautiful, with large brown eyes, long dark hair and matching sequined T-shirts.

The little girl speaks in Spanish-accented English.

"Who is that?" she asks the woman.

"We don't know her," the woman replies, and they leave.

I enter the stall and close the door, trying not to cry as I think of my own childhood.

My mother died shortly after Clay and I married but I didn't attend her funeral. My brother and sister, who adored her, were angry and stopped speaking to me. They didn't understand that as the oldest, I was charged with taking care of them as well as my mother, who neglected my own growth and development. Years later when Clay and I split up, the only person left to console me was Eva, and she told me I needed to move on.

"Life isn't easy," she coaxed during one particularly difficult period. "When you fall off the horse, Katie, you have to get back on it and ride."

Midway through dinner, Andrew drops steak on his shirt. Within seconds, the maître d' runs over and sprays it with stain remover and immediately brushes it off. Andrew pushes his hand away.

"Thanks, but no thanks," he says as the server's smile tightens.

"I'm sorry, sir," says the server, "but this should help the stain." He looks at Lola and she says something to him in Spanish.

"It's OK," she tells Andrew, "I can have my dry cleaner take care of it for you, don't worry."

"No," says Andrew, wiping the stain with his napkin, "I'll take care of it when we get home. But what the hell was he thinking?" The server moves away and I feel sorry for him.

"He was only trying to help," I say loudly enough so he can hear.

"Whatever," says Andrew, tossing his napkin to the floor. "Let's just eat our dinner, OK?" I recognize his tone and try to change the subject. Eva leans over and whispers in my ear.

"I'm going to tell you again, Kate. He's a jerk."

After Andrew and I return to our room at the hotel I confront him.

"What's going on that you're in such a bad mood?" I ask.

"It's nothing, Kate," he says. "Let it go."

I walk over to him and touch his arm.

"Andrew, something's going on. What is it? I don't understand why you're angry."

He pulls away and begins to unbutton his shirt.

"It's nothing," he says again, "let's just go to bed."

CHAPTER 3
FEEL

Our flight to San Martín de los Andes is two hours long, and we're scheduled to arrive at noon. Andrew sits by the window and naps wearing headphones, so I chat with Eva who's sitting nearby. She and Jason are holding hands.

"Andrew angry at you again?" asks Eva, leaning close.

"I'm not sure," I reply, "he's in another one of his bad moods. I thought this trip would make him happy."

"Ignore him," she says before leaning back and closing her eyes. "Just ignore him."

The day before we left Chicago, Andrew's mood improved. When I pointed it out, he said, "Fly-fishing is Zen, I think of nothing else." For weeks he had spent hours in his study with the door closed. When I asked him why, he denied there was a problem, and thus I chose to spend more time at work. Gus took notice.

"What's up with you, Kate?" he asked late one night while eating a stale bagel. He was sitting at his desk, his feet crossed on top with its usual stack of newspapers pushed aside to make room.

"You and the lawyer not getting along?"

I slapped his leg as I walked past him. "Nope, we're good," I replied, heading to my own desk, "It's just that I love spending time here with you."

When our plane lands at Chapelco Airport, the passengers applaud and I join them. Then, after pulling my purse from under the seat, I nudge Andrew to wake him. He opens his eyes, smiles and kisses me on the cheek.

"Hello, beautiful!" he says. Surprised, I happily squeeze his arm.

The flight attendant opens the cabin door and warm air fills the plane. Lining up with the other passengers, we disembark down a steep metal staircase before entering the terminal, which is just yards away. Jason and Eva walk off to find a luggage cart while Andrew and I wait for our bags.

"Are you excited?" he asks with his arm around my shoulders.

"Yes, I am," I say, watching for our bags. "You?"

"Yep," he says, picking up my duffel as it winds its way around the carousel. "Yes, I am."

After we retrieve our bags, our fishing guide, Mike, who owns a local outfitter, meets us in the terminal. He's American, short and muscular, with a long gray beard and sparkling blue eyes.

"*¡Hola!*" he shouts as he strides over to us. "Welcome to

Patagonia!"

He pulls our bags onto a luggage cart and leads us outside. We follow him to his truck and he speaks to a man wearing a khaki fishing shirt. The man approaches us, removes his sunglasses and smiles at me. I stop and stare and catch my breath. Never in my life have I seen a more beautiful man. He's slender and tall with a neat dark beard and mustache, large green eyes and perfect white teeth. His wavy brown hair, shiny and just long enough to graze his collar, is casually stuffed into a green fishing cap; his skin, tan from the sun, is the color of caramel.

Mike introduces us.

"Kate, this is Nico. Nico, this is Kate." I want to shake Nico's hand but can't since I'm carrying two small bags. He takes them from me, smiles and speaks. His voice is deep and mellow and I'm instantly smitten.

"*Buenas tardes* (Good afternoon), Kate," he says, "nice to meet you."

As Nico carries my bags to his truck, I follow him like an eager puppy. It's then that Andrew decides I'm riding with Mike.

"Jason and I are in this truck," he says, glancing at Nico as he walks over to me. "You and Eva ride with Mike."

Jason walks over and climbs into the back seat.

"Let's go fishing!" he announces, slamming the door and waving through the window. I walk to Mike's truck and stand next to Eva.

"He's cute," she says, looking at Nico.

"Let's go, ladies!" Mike yells. We hop in his truck and Eva sits in front. We speed from the airport on a narrow dirt road and I look back to see Nico's truck, but dust obstructs my view. Settling in my seat I see a tall blue sign out the window that displays a large photo of a downhill skier and states, *Región Patagonia, Argentina, Provincia del Neuquén, Bienvenidos.* I smile as I put on my sunglasses. I can hardly believe that I'm here. Scanning the countryside, I'm surprised to see that Patagonia looks a little like Wyoming where I attended summer horseback riding camp as a kid.

I mention this to Mike and he smiles at me through the rearview mirror.

"Both are deserts because we are at similar latitudes," he explains. "We are at 40.1667 degrees here, and Casper, Wyoming, is 42.8347 degrees. That's where I'm from."

I laugh and Eva gasps.

"Wow!" she exclaims. "I'm impressed that you know that much detail! Wyoming is beautiful! Why are you here?"

Mike adjusts his fishing cap before answering.

"I fell in love," he replies, "my wife is Argentine." I ponder this for several seconds, wondering how he feels about living so far from home. He changes the subject by asking if I've ever fished.

"Yes," I tell him, rolling down the window a couple of inches to let in the fresh air. "But only once."

Eva turns and looks at me.

"Nope, not once!" she declares. Mike laughs.

"Well, ladies," he says, "get ready. You're about to learn!"

As we drive I think of my father and how much he would have loved to fish in Patagonia. Having read about Argentina before our trip, I learned that the country's trout were introduced in the early 1900s by explorer Francisco Moreno. As an engineer who enjoyed details, my father would have loved to speculate how that happened, whether the fish eggs were on ice or simply sloshing around in saltwater. He would ask the fishing guides here, "Then how did they breed?" leaning forward in his eagerness to understand. He would soak up the information about catching those trout: what flies to use, what rods were best, then he would happily share stories about his own fishing adventures on Lake Michigan. My father loved to talk, but since my mother never listened, he would mostly talk to me. Over the years I learned that he was a kind and gentle man, and that fishing was his way of tuning out the world. He never traveled out of the U.S. and would have enjoyed this exotic land and his freedom to explore.

An hour from the airport we turn off the main road and drive through an open metal gate. The dirt road ahead is lined with giant poplar trees.

"Ha!" Eva bursts out. "It looks like those trees were planted just to greet us!"

We drive for a quarter mile, then stop in front of a large stone building. As Mike jumps out of the truck, I gather my bags from the back seat and open the door. A small shaggy dog, barking and leaping just a few feet from the truck, greets us as a tall woman with long dark hair gracefully walks through the front door. She's wearing a colorful caftan and boots and strides over to greet us.

"*¡Hola!* Welcome!" she says, hugging me as Eva steps out of the truck. "I'm Lara, how was your trip?" Before I can answer, Nico's truck drives up behind us and stops. Andrew steps out and waves at me, then walks to the back of the truck to retrieve our gear. Nico climbs out, shuts his door and looks at me. I turn to join Lara and Eva as they walk to the lodge, but before I do, I pause to smile at Nico and he smiles back.

Lara leads us to our rooms, all the while explaining in Spanish-accented English that the lodge is part of a giant sheep ranch. She says that in Spanish, the word for "ranch" is *estancia* and I repeat it, noting with amusement that in English the word has only one syllable whereas in Spanish it has four.

I mention this to Lara and she laughs.

"Yes," she says, "we have a way of expressing the same things as you, only it takes us longer!"

As she continues to walk, she tells us that the estancia is named Salida del Sol, which means sunrise in Spanish. It extends over 130,000 acres, is 100 years old and is home to nearly 20,000 sheep, which, she says with a smile, are "nearly naked" since they were just sheared in December. Nearby are the Chimehuin and Quilquihue Rivers where we will fish.

"But here we don't use the word 'river,'" explains Lara. "We say in Spanish *río* for river. So it's the *Río* Chimehuin and *Río* Quilquihue."

As we walk into the living room, I smell vanilla.

"It's because of the candles," Lara relates over her shoulder as we pass the kitchen. A server walks by with a basket of what look like tiny pillows made of pastry. Lara stops to check them.

"Empanadas," she says, nodding to the server. "They're yours. You're having lunch on the river."

Our room is spacious with a queen-sized bed, numerous decorative pillows and flower vases filled with fresh lilacs. The large windows are open and a gentle breeze billows the white curtains into the room. I peek outside and am pleased to see a flower garden and patio with chairs and a picnic table. A server is setting the table for lunch.

"All the comforts of home," I murmur.

I head to the bathroom where there's a large walk-in shower, white claw-foot tub and giant basket filled with bath salts and lotions. I turn to find Andrew and see that he's pulling fishing gear out of his duffel.

"I love this!" I cry, reaching for my suitcase. Andrew is silent so I begin to unpack my clothes.

"Are you ready to go?" he asks. "The truck is waiting for us."

I turn to look at him. I want to object to his bossiness, but instead I sigh. I pull a jacket from the suitcase and lay it on the bed. When Andrew sees it, he tells me that I won't need it.

"It will just get in the way in the boat," he explains. "If you get cold you can wear mine."

When I first met Andrew, we were waiting for a taxi outside the courthouse where I had been covering a trial for our local newspaper. He was the defense attorney and his case was going well. It was freezing outside. The temperature had dropped nearly 10 degrees since that morning, and I had forgotten my coat.

"You can borrow mine," Andrew said, wrapping it around my shoulders. "Just give it back to me tomorrow."

Since he was in a jubilant mood, he asked if I wanted to get a drink. As a married woman I said no, but he insisted, and since Clay was out of town, I finally agreed. We climbed into a taxi together and had dinner at his favorite Italian restaurant. We talked for hours about the trial, his recent separation from his wife and my devotion to journalism. I told him I wanted to make a difference and he accused me of being an idealistic cub reporter. His cynicism stung.

"Trust me," he said, "the world is a dangerous place. It will take an act of God to save it."

When we finally parted, I arrived home and realized I was still wearing his jacket. Lending a coat is something my father would have done, I thought as I hung it in my closet, except that he would have told me to keep it.

As we drive to the river, I sit in the back seat of Mike's truck and listen as he and Andrew talk about fishing. Sun is pouring through the windows, so I dig into my orange fishing bag, pull out my new pink fishing cap and put it on along with my new purple Maui Jim sunglasses. As I look out the window I see a herd of animals in the distance and ask Mike what they are.

"Guanacos," he replies, "they look like llamas, don't they?" I nod and as we pass them, they turn their heads to watch us. "They're all over," he adds, "but they seem to know not to run in the road. Not like deer in the U.S."

A few miles later I see a snow-covered, cone-shaped mountain sitting alone in the distance. I ask Andrew if he knows what it is and he shakes his head.

"Lanín," says Mike. "It's a dormant volcano on the border of Argentina and Chile." Then smiling, he adds, "We don't really know the last time it erupted, but we're hoping that it's not in the next two weeks, during your visit."

We drive through a gate to get to the Chimehuin River where we're going to fish. Before getting to the water, we travel for nearly 30 minutes down a deeply rutted winding gravel road as our fishing rods, attached to a carrier on the front of the truck, jump and rattle. I look at Andrew, waiting for him to get angry, and in a few moments, he does.

"I paid thousands of dollars for those rods," he curtly informs Mike.

"Ouch, I'm sorry!" Mike responds before he jumps from the truck. He removes the rods, takes them apart and hands them to

Andrew.

"Thanks, man," says Andrew. "Sorry that I got angry."

"No problem," says Mike. "If they were my rods, I would be angry, too."

I am amused by this exchange. Andrew has never apologized to me.

Twenty minutes later we arrive at the river and park on the bank. Eva walks over to me and tells me she needs to pee.

"I don't see any bathrooms here," she says sarcastically, looking around. "Remind me again why I decided to come here."

As she's talking, I realize I need to pee, too.

"You go there and I'll go over here," I tell her, pointing to giant bushes in the distance. "See you in a few."

While heading to my spot, I hear movement to my left. I look and see a cow and her calf meandering nearby.

"Uh-oh, cow poop," I whisper, looking down and tiptoeing around large piles of dung. When I finally step behind the bushes and look up, I gasp. Stretching in front of me are acres and acres of tall yellow grass, shimmering like gold in the mid-afternoon sun.

"Beautiful," I whisper again as I unzip my fishing pants. I pull a small wad of toilet paper from my shirt pocket and kneel down. The grass tickles my bottom and I giggle.

"Gus," I whisper, "this potty break is for you."

When I return to the river I watch Mike and Nico as they launch the boats. Each boat is made of fiberglass and has three seats; between the seats are coolers and giant waterproof duffels that are full of flies, fishing line and other essential gear. Leg braces are attached to the front and back of the boat in case we want to stand while fishing.

Andrew insists that I sit in the front because he wants to coach me.

"Remember, ten and two," he instructs as he rigs his rod. I thank him, and as I slather sunscreen on my face and arms I watch Nico, who's chatting with Eva. I wonder if he's married or has a girlfriend, but I'm too shy to ask. I figure he speaks limited English, but in a minute I learn that I'm wrong.

"Eva wants to fish with you," he says to me, wading to our boat, "she says you're an expert." I take off my sunglasses to look at him.

"I'm hardly an expert," I respond, "but I'm happy to help." I swing around to look at Andrew, who's still rigging his rod.

"That's fine," he says, "I'll help Jason. You go help Eva."

Nico extends his hand to help me climb from the boat, and when my fingers touch his they tingle. The sensation is so powerful and unexpected that I nearly fall to my knees. Nico gently grabs my arm.

"You OK?" he asks, and I look at him, embarrassed. What was that tingling? Did he feel it, too?

"I'm fine," I answer, looking down. Then, remembering my rudimentary Spanish, I add, "*gracias*, Nico, *muchas gracias*."

I sit in the back of the boat and Eva sits in front, swiveling her chair to face Nico so she can grill him for details. I learn that he's single, lives alone and has been a fishing guide for eight years. He ties his own flies, enjoys biking in the Andes and teaches skiing during the winter. He likes art and fine food, has five brothers and two sisters and his mother teaches English at the local high school. After he tells Eva that his family's ancestry is Italian, his grandparents having moved from Sicily to Argentina in 1920, she cries, "My family is Italian, too! *Impressionante*!" and then leans over to tell me, "That means awesome in Italian."

We drift for several minutes as I cast over and over, my fly landing in various places without hooking a fish. Nico is watching this even as he talks to Eva, and he tells me to "put more power" in my back cast. Eager to please him, I whip the rod back and pull it forward, but my fly gets stuck in my cap. He leans over to remove it and his hand grazes my neck. I gasp and feel myself blush.

"It's OK, Kate," he says as he quickly plucks the fly from the rim. "I got it. You're free."

Between casts I sightsee and am especially intrigued by the tall plants with draping white plumes. When the wind blows, they shimmer.

"Pampas grass," explains Nico when I ask what they are.

After a few minutes of silence, Eva asks him if he wants to visit the U.S. and he tells her that yes, he just got his visa, but that he would avoid the big cities, including Chicago.

"The big cities are too complicated," he explains. They discuss the wonders of the American West and Eva commits to showing him Yellowstone one day. I listen to all of this while I try to hook a fish, and on what seems like my hundredth cast, I finally do.

"Fish!" I yell, "fish!"

Nico quickly drops the anchor and picks up his net. As I try to pull the fish to the boat, he calmly gives me instructions.

"You don't have to rush, Kate, just take your time."

I turn to him and out of the corner of my eye see Andrew waving in the distance.

"Nice job!" he shouts. "Hold your rod tip high!"

As I wave back, Nico speaks.

"Just let him run," he says, and for a moment, I think he's talking about Andrew.

CHAPTER 4

LAUGH

Lunch that day is on the riverbank. Nico and Mike pull a folded table from the boat along with four green chairs and two blue coolers. They assemble our dining area beneath a large clump of willows and begin to unpack the food.

Eva and I sit facing the river, and she pulls a small container of hand sanitizer from her vest.

"OK, Kate," she says, "how in the heck did you learn to fish like that?" She squeezes a large drop of sanitizer on my palm.

"It was Andrew," I answer, "and a lot of luck."

Nico, who's listening, walks over and smiles.

"I don't think it was luck, Kate," he says, placing a container of green olives in front of me. I pop one in my mouth. It tastes cold and salty.

"Ah-love olives!" I cry. "*¡Gracias!*" He removes his sunglasses and smiles.

"*De nada*," he responds. His eyes rest on me and linger before he turns away. I swallow the olive and watch him as he continues to unpack our food.

As we eat, I learn that Nico has a girlfriend. Her name is

Marina and she owns a popular dance studio in town. They grew up together and began dating as teens, but split when Nico left for college. Two years later, Marina dislocated her right shoulder while setting up a dance recital. The surgeon who fixed her shoulder injured a nerve and Marina lost the use of her arm. Nico returned home to help her, and never returned to college.

"Hey, Nico, how's Marina?" asks Mike as he sits down to lunch.

"Good," says Nico, slicing cheese and sausage onto a platter for the group. "She wanted to come to the *asado* tomorrow, but I told her it wasn't necessary."

Jason looks up from his plate.

"As-what-o?" he asks.

Mike sits down and pulls three empanadas from a plastic container before passing it to Andrew.

"It's a barbeque," he explains, taking a bite from the empanada. It's stuffed with meat. "We're camping on the river tomorrow night. You OK with that?"

"That's awesome!" says Jason with his mouth full of food. "Eva and I love to camp out!"

Eva turns and looks at him, feigning shock.

"Sorry?" she asks. "Which Eva are you talking about?" Jason grins and nudges her with his elbow.

"That would be you," he says. "My Eva diva."

When we return to the boats it's midafternoon. Eva sits in front and I doze in the back, but I awaken when she screams, "Fish!" Opening my eyes, I watch as Nico jumps up to help Eva with her rod. Something is pulling it under the boat.

"Fish!" she screams again. "At least I think it's a fish! Where's it going?"

Nico shouts, "Rod tip up!" and drops the anchor with one hand while picking up his net with the other. "Rod tip up!"

I remember what Andrew taught me – that if you pull too hard on the line the fish will break off – so I yell to Eva.

"Let it run, let it run!"

Eva stands from her chair, steadies herself against the leg brace and holds the rod over her head. The reel makes a high-pitched sound as it releases the line and the rod shivers as the fish darts in every direction.

"Don't let it go under the boat!" Nico shouts, and Eva nods her head. The boat rocks side to side as she turns slowly to manage the fish, and minutes later she reels it in. Nico scoops it into the net. After releasing it, he gives her a high-five before they both sit down. He opens the cooler, reaches inside and hands each of us a bottle of water.

"What a team!" she squeals as Nico begins to row. "This is *impressionante*! I could learn to like this!"

As the day grows late I watch Nico as he rows and fantasize about rubbing his back. His muscular shoulders pull his shirt tight as he leans forward with each row. When he moves backward, I slouch in my chair to move my knees forward, hoping that they will touch him. I begin to feel hypnotized by his movements and stare at his wavy hair as it moves around on his collar. I smile when I see a few freckles on his neck and wish I could kiss them. What would he taste like? As he speaks to Eva, I delight in his accented English and am both soothed and aroused by his deep mellow voice.

Since Mike's boat is nowhere in sight, we're alone on this stretch of river and Nico acts like a tour guide.

"Ladies," he says, "over there, look at that willow tree, its roots are growing out of the bank."

"Really?" asks Eva. "Are you sure it's a willow?"

"Yep," he replies with a nod, "it's definitely a willow and you can bank on that." I groan.

He tells Eva that the small bushes on the bank are called neneos.

"No way!" she declares. "They're sagebrush!"

I laugh. Eva always plays the cynic and I'm grateful that she's here. After a few minutes, she asks Nico if she can watch him fish.

"Sure," he says, lowering the anchor, "but just for a minute."

She hands him her rod, and I stare at her, admiring her boldness, while Nico pulls extra line from the reel. In a flash, he casts the line and I watch as it makes a perfect loop, stretches dozens of yards toward the shoreline, and falls gently to the water. The fly, appearing from this distance like a tuft of white, bobs slowly along the bank and within moments is grabbed by a fish. Eva and I look at each other in amazement as Nico lands and releases the fish, casts again and accomplishes another perfect loop, another perfect line, another perfect landing. His technique seems effortless and is awe-inspiring, like a ballerina on point or a pianist playing Brahms. It's at this moment that I fully understand the art of fly-fishing, but since I'm struggling for words to express it, Eva speaks first.

"Wow, Nico, where did you learn to cast like that?"

He laughs and hands the rod back to her.

"Practice makes perfect," he says, pulling the anchor up as he begins to row. "Someday you could cast like that, too." As Eva scoffs and they continue to chat, I close my eyes so that I can seal the memory of Nico fishing. It occurs to me that I haven't thought of Andrew all day, but I don't care. Instead, I close my eyes as our boat, rocking like a cradle, drifts slowly and smoothly toward home.

At dusk we see the trucks in the distance and I'm sad that our day has ended. I begin to gather my gear when Nico yells "Hey!" at a young man standing on the bank holding a stringer of fish. The man turns and runs and Nico quickly drops the anchor as he pulls a VHF radio from his pocket.

"Poacher," he explains to Eva and me, "I'm calling Fish and Game."

After speaking to someone in Spanish, he puts the radio back in his pocket and the young man runs away.

"He was probably catching fish to sell at a restaurant," he explains as he continues to row. "I called the authorities and they will find him. He shouldn't be killing the fish."

When my father fished in Lake Michigan, he always returned home empty-handed and it drove my mother nuts.

"Bob," she said each time, "do you catch any fish at all? What are you doing out there?"

He would wink at me and smile before saying, "I catch a lot of fish, but I release them. That way, they grow bigger and bigger and I can catch them again next summer."

My mother rolled her eyes and walked away, but I followed him outside to help him clean out his boat.

"Kate," he said, "one day I'll teach you how to fish and you can go with me. The fish are beautiful and they swim and swim and swim. Sometimes you can see them play beneath the surface."

I asked him where they were going and he picked me up to give me a hug. "Nowhere special," he said, "just enjoying their freedom. And don't tell your mom, but that's why I release them."

Dinner is late and we eat with Lara. Animated and beautiful, wearing a white turtleneck and red-beaded necklace, she sits at the head of the table and describes Patagonia. She speaks in perfect English with a charming Spanish accent and is extraordinarily warm and personable. I feel like I've known her forever.

"The roads here are terrible!" she complains, passing bread with one hand and gesturing wildly with the other. "You know, we pave them, but then the rain and snow come. And since they're not graded it's no use; they're still terrible."

"That's my area," Jason chimes in as he refills his wine glass, "I'm a general contractor. Is there good equipment?"

Then Andrew interrupts.

"Let's talk about something else, do you mind? Like fishing?" I look down at my plate. I recognize that he's inebriated and squirm in my chair.

"Of course!" says Lara, "how was your day today?" Andrew's face brightens.

"Good!" he declares, "we caught a 21-inch brown!"

Jason leans over the table to give him a high-five.

"Way to go, buddy!" he says.

Though I'm happy for Andrew, I miss Nico and Mike. They returned to town before dinner and will pick us up in the morning.

"Eva caught a fish today," I tell the group, "it was awesome." Eva laughs.

"Nothing like Katie," she says, "Katie's quite a fisherwoman."

"Yep," says Andrew. "She's on fire."

"Speaking of fire," says Lara, clearing our plates, "you know that Mike and Nico are taking you camping tomorrow night."

"Yep," says Jason, standing up, "I'm going to bed. I want to be ready for the upside-down-o."

I laugh. Hard.

"*Asado*," laughs Lara as she carries the dishes to the kitchen. "By the way, you'll also meet Marina, Nico's girlfriend. She called today and said she will be joining you."

I stop laughing.

We fish the next day from dawn until dusk. Because Andrew insisted that we fish with Mike, I don't see Nico, Eva or Jason until we row to the campsite. When we arrive, Nico is unpacking their boat and Jason is standing knee deep in the river admiring the tents that Rubén, our *asador*, set up earlier.

"Nice!" he calls out, swatting mosquitoes with his cap. "Eva, you're sleeping out here with the bugs, right?"

She climbs from their boat and gives him a kiss before gently punching him on the arm.

"No, honey, I'm sleeping in the tent with you!"

I watch them, wistful, as they walk hand-in-hand to their tent. I want a relationship like theirs: committed and kind, playful and trusting. Andrew and Mike follow, carrying our duffels. When they're out of sight, Nico wades over to me.

"Kate," he says, "Marina will be here this evening."

I look at him and smile. Why is he telling me?

"I know, Nico," I respond as I take off my cap. My hair, tucked inside, cascades down my back, and I begin to pull it into a ponytail. "Lara told us last night. That's great!"

"All right then," he replies, picking up one of the coolers. As he carries it up the bank I watch him, wondering what it would be like to sleep with him under the stars.

After I gather my gear from the boat, I walk to our tent past an expansive ground fire that's set inside four logs. In the middle are two metal crosses strung with large roasting carcasses.

"What is this?" I ask, staring.

"*Cordero*," explains Rubén as he walks over to me. "It means lamb in Spanish. We're also having chorizo. Do you like lamb?"

"*¡Sí!*" I exclaim as Eva joins me. She's already changed clothes.

"Cool," she says, "I've seen these in pictures. When do we eat?"

"When Marina gets here," shouts Mike, and I feel my stomach jump.

Though Andrew and I live together, I don't know if I love him, and one day I mentioned this to Gus. We were drinking coffee in the newsroom an hour before deadline and as usual, Gus had his feet on top of his desk. I was sitting on the other side watching him as he kept checking his computer to see if the copy editors were finished with my story.

"There's just no passion there," I said, nervously wrapping a long strand of hair around my finger. "I mean, we're comfortable with each other and I know he would never cheat on me. At least, I don't think he would."

Gus turned to stare at me.

"Kate, are you serious? A beautiful girl like you settling for 'I know he would never cheat on me?' Look," he continued, leaning toward me with his elbows on his knees, "what's love anyway? I mean, you were married once and I've been married once. Wouldn't it be nice if we could all just have sex? Just enjoy the moment."

I laughed. Gus is like a father to me, protective and predictable. He's also occasionally outrageous.

"Ha!" I laughed, "that will work. What happens when that moment is over?" I waited for Gus to answer but instead he looked at the computer, shouted "Done!" and leapt from his chair.

"Kate," he said, drinking the last of his coffee before throwing the cup into the trash, "you need to take your time before getting involved again. Find someone who makes you happy. Life is just too damn short to be sad."

Rubén has built a campfire near the roasting lamb and we gather around it to share stories about our day. Andrew and Jason have caught several large rainbows and are bragging about their conquests. Eva is asking Rubén how to marinate the lamb and whether he likes chicken.

"No, are you kidding?" he responds. "Only people in the U.S. like chicken." Then he passes a plate of empanadas and a large platter of cheese, spicy ham, chorizo and blood sausages, and olives. Nico, who's standing nearby, pours Malbec into our plastic wine glasses and sips on a beer. Soon we hear a car in the distance and he turns to walk to the road.

Marina drives up in a compact red Citroën and parks beneath a tree. When she climbs from the car Nico greets her with a hug and leads her over to meet us. She's petite and slender with light brown hair and is wearing an orange fleece jacket, blue jeans and boots.

"*¡Hola!*" she says as she walks over. "*¿Cómo estás?* How are you?"

"*¡Hola!*" we reply as we all stand up. Jason gestures for her to sit next to him.

"Thank you!" she says as she sits down. "You must be Andrew?"

"Nope," he says, "I'm Jason, that's Andrew." Andrew waves and then points to me. "And that's Kate," he says. Eva waves.

"And I'm her best friend Eva; we're very glad you could join us!"

Marina smiles and with her left hand places her right arm across her lap. I wonder how she's doing.

We chat for several minutes about her dance studio as I watch Nico and Rubén prepare dinner. She doesn't speak to them and when I ask her if she likes to fish, she smiles.

"No," she responds.

Mike, who is adding wood to the fire, asks about her arm.

"It's getting better," she says, rubbing it. "I'm working with a therapist three days a week but there's still a long way to go."

Mike pokes the fire with a stick and as it sparks, he moves back.

"You should try fly-fishing," he says, glancing at me. "Casting will make your arm stronger. Just ask Kate." Marina laughs.

"That's what Nico tells me," she says, "but I don't like to fish."

The lamb is served at a picnic table along with large bowls of *ensalada rusa*, Argentine potato salad. We eat heartily, talk about fishing and drink more Malbec. Marina tells us that she's lived in San Martín de los Andes her entire life and that her father is the city's mayor. She has five brothers, three sisters and 120 cousins; all, she says, live nearby. I watch Nico as she speaks and he seems distant; when his eyes meet mine he looks away.

After dinner we share yerba maté, a tea-like drink that is prepared and served in a calabash gourd. In Argentina, it's customary in a social gathering to drink from the same gourd through a decorative metal straw called a bombilla. We do that tonight, though Andrew chooses not to.

"Oh come on, Andrew," says Eva, who I can tell is inebriated. "It's not going to hurt you."

Andrew glares at her and frowns.

"Leave him alone," says Jason, looking at Andrew, who's sitting next to him. "He doesn't have to partake, right buddy?" He extends his hand to Andrew for a fist bump, but Andrew waves it away.

"Thanks," he says, "you don't need to speak for me. The caffeine will keep me awake."

Eva moves to Jason and sits on his lap.

"Oh baloney, Andrew," she says. "You're just a snob, admit it." Jason puts his hand over her mouth.

Andrew says nothing and Marina speaks as if to soothe tempers.

"No problem," she says, "my brothers don't even like maté that much. They prefer coffee."

Mike laughs as he takes the gourd from Jason who has just taken a long sip.

"Maté takes some getting used to," he says, "but that's all I drink now. It celebrates relationships. I didn't get that at first, but now I do."

Eva gives Jason a kiss on the cheek.

"Hear! Hear!" she says, as Nico stands from the table and begins to clear the dishes. I watch him and wonder if he's always this quiet. What is he like? What makes him worry? What makes him laugh?

A few minutes later, Marina says goodnight.

"You're not staying?" Eva asks.

"No," she answers, "I teach classes in the morning. Good night everyone! *¡Que duerman bien!* (Sleep well)." As Nico walks her to her car, Eva and I clear the table. Jason and Andrew move to sit at the fire, which is now just a field of glowing embers.

"Well, she's beautiful," says Eva, scraping food scraps into a bag. "I hope her arm gets better."

"Me, too," I say, gathering the wine glasses to put them in the washtub, "but she doesn't fish. That's odd."

"No it's not," says Eva. "Some would say it's odd that we fish."

I say nothing for a minute then tell her I'm tired.

"I'm going to sleep," I yawn, then walk to Andrew to kiss him goodnight. "See you in the morning."

Andrew stands, stretches, tells Jason goodnight, and follows me to the tent. Inside we undress and slip into our sleeping bags, and a minute later, he's snoring. Since I can't sleep, I pull on my pants and walk outside. Rubén and Eva are chatting at the picnic table and I head to the river.

Nico is sitting on a blue cooler at the bank. He gestures for me to sit with him and I do, stuffing my hands into my pockets. He puts his elbows on his knees and looks at me.

"Can't sleep?" he asks. I look at the river and wait for a moment before responding,

"Nope, must be the wine."

"Wine puts most people to sleep," he says, "not you?" I'm amused by our small talk; what do we say when it's not about fishing? I feel his jacket brush against mine and know that our hips are nearly touching. I wonder if he knows that, too.

Nico and I talk about Patagonia and Chicago. He wants to know if I like being a journalist.

"A lot of the time it sucks," I tell him. "There's so much crime to write about in the city, we could fill a dozen pages every day. That's why I'm doing features."

He picks up a rock and skips it across the water; it bounces three times then hits the opposite bank.

"The city's complicated," he says, "when I lived in Buenos Aires I hated it. So many people, so much going on. That's why I live here."

I pick up a rock and throw it at the water; it skips once and then sinks.

"I want to visit a tango show before we go home," I tell him. "Do you tango?"

He pauses for a second and picks up a stick. As he rolls it between his palms, he smiles and looks at me.

"Nope, I do not tango."

Since he's smiling I wonder if he's joking.

"Why?" I ask.

"Well, first of all," he says, "I'm not a tango kind of guy." I'm confused.

"What do you mean?" I ask. "What's a tango kind of guy?"

"It's someone who likes to hang out in the city," he says, tossing the stick into the water, "and I really don't like the city."

I look up to the sky and see the moon between the trees. Nearly full it seems close and casts yellow light on the river. We're sitting near a quiet pool and hear the river in the distance. I look at the water and a ring interrupts its glassy surface. It emanates then dissipates and the pool is once again calm.

"A rise," says Nico. "The fish must be eating."

We talk about his love of fishing.

"I enjoy the challenge," he says, "just like you. And no matter where you fish in the world, whether it's here, the U.S. or Russia, we all want the same thing, and that's to catch that fish."

He stretches his legs in front of him and crosses his arms.

"It brings us together," he continues, "like the fish and the fly. It's the most basic connection. As a guide, helping my client achieve that connection is the best feeling in the world."

He looks at me and pauses before continuing. I'm fighting the urge to kiss him.

"In fishing it's called the 'set,'" he explains, "when all the work that comes before is put to the test." He picks up another rock and throws it at the river. It lands on the opposite bank.

"Tell me about Marina," I say, clasping my hands.

Nico is still looking at the river and waits a moment before answering.

"She needs me," he says, "you know, because of her arm." Several seconds pass before he continues.

"She doesn't want me to guide any more," he adds. "She claims it takes too much time away from her."

He sounds sad and I feel protective.

"That doesn't make sense," I tell him. "She must know that you love what you do."

"She does," he answers, standing. I look up and see his silhouette. His face is hidden by the dark, but the moon backlights his wavy hair so that it looks like a halo.

"Then she could fish with you," I say. "It would help her arm to get strong."

"Women here don't fish," he says as he leans over and picks up a rock. He rubs it on his shirt and places it in my palm. "They aren't like you."

The rock is the size of a walnut and I wrap my fingers around it. I want to stand and hug him but he speaks instead.

"It's time for bed, Kate," he says, walking toward camp. "We'll start early in the morning. Sleep well."

I sit on the cooler for a few more minutes, then return to the tent. I place the rock carefully atop my waders and snuggle into my bag. Andrew's still snoring, and as I drift to sleep I think of our *asado*, maté and Nico.

I awake the next morning to voices and the aroma of coffee. I look for Andrew, but his sleeping bag is empty so I jump up and get dressed. The sun shines through the tent and I reach for my rock, but it's not there. I shake my waders and sleeping bag and check my jacket pockets. When I still can't find it, I pull on my pants, comb my hair, slip on my Crocs, and walk outside. I wonder if last night was simply a dream.

Andrew is near our tent and greets me.

"Good morning, sleepy head!" he says cheerfully. "Coffee for you?" I nod yes and look for Nico.

"Breakfast is over there," he continues, taking my hand. "Rubén has cooked bacon and eggs."

I follow Andrew and see Nico at the river loading the boats. Mike is with him and their conversation, all in Spanish, is punctuated by laughter. Patagonia is beautiful in the morning. I marvel at the mist on the water and the birds screaming in the distance. The air is chilly so I zip up my fleece to cover my neck. I'm eager to fish so I hurriedly scoop eggs onto my plate and butter a thick slice of bread. Rubén brings me fresh bacon and orange juice, and as I eat, I hear Eva and Jason in their tent. They're talking about condors.

"No," says Jason, sounding exasperated, "those aren't condors, they're smaller birds. Condors are huge. I saw them on TV. They have giant wingspans and white collars like they're wearing shirts and going to work." When I hear Eva laugh, I smile.

Then Andrew shows me my rock.

"I found this in the tent," he says, holding it between two fingers. "You didn't mean to bring it in there, did you?" I watch as he throws it at the river, but it lands several yards away on a tall bush. I run to the bush and climb between its thorny branches to retrieve it, but it's out of reach.

"Hey," Andrew continues, picking up his boots, "Jason and I will fish with Nico today. You and Eva fish with Mike, OK?"

I stare at him; I wonder if he senses my feelings about Nico.

"Sure," I reply, taking a bite of eggs, "whatever you say."

"Great!" he says, walking to the tent.

I watch and sip my coffee and see Eva emerge from her tent. I gesture her over.

"*Buenos dias,*" she says sleepily, rubbing her eyes. "Did you sleep well?"

"Yes, you?" I reply. But I'm not paying attention to her.

Instead, I'm watching Nico.

CHAPTER 5

SOAR

After Mike helps me into his boat, I wave goodbye to Andrew and worry that he won't be nice to Nico. Powerless, I relax in my seat and decide that Nico can handle it. I scan the river, looking for fish, but they're hard to find. Wild fish are adept at surviving and frequently hide among a river's mottled rocks. To conserve energy, they lie with their heads pointing upstream and eat insects as they unwittingly float by, sometimes emerging from the water to catch one in flight. I see one do this as Mike begins to row, and I watch, fascinated, as several more do the same. Because there are so many fish, the water looks like it's beginning to boil, and I squeal with delight.

"Look at them!" I shout to Eva. "Can you believe this? There must be 50 fish out there!" Mike laughs.

"There you go, Kate," he says quietly. "Pull out some line and cast about 10 feet, but be careful not to scare the fish." I do as instructed and my fly, called a purple haze, lands gently on the water's surface.

"Nice cast," he says, continuing to row, "now strip in some line."

I strip slowly, recast and am surprised to see my fly disappear beneath the surface. My line, once relaxed on the water like a serpent, shivers and is pulled tight by an unseen force that drags it into a grove of willows that are growing out of the water.

"Fish!" I cry, laughing at its ingenuity to hide. Holding my rod tip high, I pull hard to get it out. Eva is screaming at me.

"Oh my God, Kate, oh my God! It's huge! Don't let this one go!" The fish does feel heavy, but I've learned that even the smallest trout can fight so hard that they seem like giants. That's the case today, as I finally pull a tiny rainbow to the boat. It seems tired, and since I'm eager to get it back into the water, I decline Mike's suggestion that he take a photo. As Mike releases it, I advise the fish to "have fun and grow up" as Nico pulls his boat alongside us.

Andrew gestures a high five.

"Nice work!" he says. "A little fighter! Did you catch that by yourself?" I smile at him, look at Nico and say nothing.

"Yes, she did," says Mike. "It swam under the willows and she still landed it."

Nico, grinning, touches the brim of his cap and gestures a salute.

"Just the first of many," he pronounces as he rows away.

That night before dinner I ask Lara about Marina. We're strolling near the lodge admiring the lilacs, which I've discovered are home to dozens of black and orange bumblebees. I watch them closely as they move from stem to stem. Their clear lacy wings are nearly invisible and their bodies are neon bright against the purple flowers.

"Marina's great isn't she?" asks Lara. "It's terrible what happened to her arm." I nod and ask what she's doing about it.

Before answering, Lara stops and speaks to a gardener who's clipping a few of the lilacs to place in decorative vases and pillows in our rooms. As we continue to walk, Lara says that Marina is undergoing physical therapy.

"I don't know if it's helping," she says, "but Nico's been taking her every week."

I stop and touch one of the bushes, feigning interest as I contemplate my next question.

"How long have they been together?"

Lara picks up an empty gum wrapper on the ground before speaking.

"Oh," she says, "don't get me started about Nico. Marina wants to get married, but he doesn't. She tells me he wants to wait until he has enough money to raise a family."

I feel a fluttering in my chest and try not to smile.

"But I'm glad you're getting to know Marina and Nico," she continues. "They're a nice couple. Let's go inside for dinner."

At dinner there's a new guest and his name is Martín. He's from Switzerland and has come to Argentina to trek. He asks me if I fish.

"Yes," I tell him, sipping my wine and looking at Andrew, who is sitting next to me. "Andrew is my instructor."

"Good for you!" Martín answers, lifting his glass as if to toast.

"Do you like it?"

Before I can respond, Andrew interrupts.

"She likes it," he says, "do you fish?"

Instead of turning to Andrew, Martín continues to smile at me.

"Nope," he says, taking a bite of salad. "But I would love to get Kate's opinion on what it's like to fish here. Are you catching anything?"

I look at him with tears in my eyes. I'm grateful that he respects my opinion and am weary of Andrew's bad mood.

"Yes!" I respond, leaning toward him. "Many rainbows and a few browns. And the guides here are wonderful!" Andrew gets up and leaves the room. Eva, who is sitting a few seats away, looks at me and rolls her eyes.

THE NEXT MORNING Eva and I decide to shop in town and Rubén is to be our guide. Andrew and Jason will fish.

"You girls have fun!" shouts Jason as they drive away in Mike's truck.

Lara has told us that Nico is at home and I wonder what he's doing. Eva tries to get my attention by linking her arm through mine and pulling me toward Rubén's truck.

"Rubén," chirps Eva, swinging her purse onto her shoulder, "where are we going?" As we climb into the truck's back seat, I tell her that Lara has mentioned a clothing shop. I try to remember the name to tell Rubén and when I stumble, he smiles.

"Yes," he says, turning the key in the ignition and winking at me in the rearview mirror. "I know it. No problem."

San Martín de los Andes is casually referred to as "the Aspen of Argentina." Full of specialty shops, its sidewalks are crowded during the autumn and many of the restaurants offer outdoor dining. Today their tables are full.

"So many tourists," says Rubén as he tries to find a parking spot. "Good for the town though."

Eva smiles and squeezes his shoulder.

"You're a man of few words Rubén," she tells him. "I like that."

After Rubén parks, we leave the car and walk across the street. He leads us to a clothing store and waits for us outside. Eva and I quickly scan the racks of shoes, boots and dresses and admire the silver jewelry that's displayed in felt-lined alcoves along the walls. I pick up an amethyst necklace and hear someone call my name. I turn and see Marina.

"Kate!" she exclaims, walking over to me. "Hello! A nice surprise! Are you buying souvenirs?" She hugs me and I hug her back. She's so thin, she feels like a child.

"This is my cousin Catalina's store," she says, resting her hand on my back. "Let me introduce you." She leads us into a back room. Catalina is sitting there with two men and they all stand as we approach.

"Kate and Eva," says Marina, "these are my brothers, Felipe and José, and my cousin, Catalina."

"Hello," I say, shaking Felipe's hand and then José's. Like Nico, they are dark and handsome, and they smile as they say, "*Buenas tardes*." Catalina takes my hand.

"Here," she says, "have you seen our new shoes? I would love to show them to you. Please follow me."

A short time later we leave the store, having bought necklaces, bracelets and scarves. Rubén is nowhere in sight, so Eva and I stop at a nearby café for lunch. We sit outside at tables with open large green umbrellas.

"OK," says Eva, dropping her bags into the empty chair, "let's figure this out." I look at her, confused. "You know," she continues, "Marina has family everywhere here. What's up with that?"

I put on my sunglasses and watch a man walk by; a young boy is perched on his shoulders and is clutching his curly dark hair. I smile and wave and the man waves back.

"She told us she was raised here. Her father's the mayor and she has a bunch of brothers. It's no big deal, she has a large family."

Even as I say it I realize I'm lying. It is a big deal. I'm beginning to have feelings for Nico and wonder how I'm going to tell Andrew and how I'll compete with Marina and her huge family.

A server approaches our table and hands us menus written in Spanish and English. I order a salad and Eva orders a pizza. When the server walks away, Eva waves and yells, "Over here!" so I look up and see Nico, wearing blue jeans and a T-shirt, as he's crossing the street. He's headed our way and I fold my arms on the table, determined not to look as excited as I am.

When he gets to the table, he takes off his sunglasses and I stare at his green eyes, which, I've decided, are the color of the finest jade. His eyelashes are long and dark. Because he's not wearing his fishing cap, I see that his wavy hair has auburn highlights and that they extend into his beard. I watch him speak as he tells us that he's meeting someone for lunch. Eva wants to know who.

"It's Marina's brother, Alex," he responds. Then he glances at our bags. "You girls shopping?"

I look up at him and smile.

"Very astute," I tell him. "We were at Marina's cousin's shop. We met two of her brothers. She has quite a family."

Nico smiles back. Eva has removed her sunglasses, is cupping her hand over her eyebrows and is squinting. She looks at him and then at me.

"Yes, she does," he says, adding, "you must mean Catalina. Listen," he says, as the server delivers our food, "I have to go. See you this afternoon?"

"This afternoon?" I ask, surprised. "Are we all having dinner?"

Nico squeezes my shoulder before walking away.

"No, but I'll be at the lodge to drop off a cooler. Maybe we could have a drink outside? I'll see you then." He disappears into the crowd.

I'm disappointed that he's left and Eva notices.

"OK, Katie," she says, crunching on a slice of pizza, "what's going on with you two?"

I blush and poke my salad with my fork.

"Nothing," I answer, adding, "well, actually, I do like him."

Eva laughs.

"No kidding!" she exclaims, wiping a blotch of red sauce from the corner of her mouth. "I think he likes you, too!"

I look at her and smile.

"You know," I tell her as I take a drink of water, "this isn't high school. We're just friends." Eva laughs and begins to speak, but I put up my hand to stop her.

"And need I remind you," I add, "I'm here with Andrew."

AFTER LUNCH we walk around town before returning to the lodge. It's 6 o'clock and Andrew and Jason haven't returned from the river.

"It's OK," says Lara reassuringly when she greets us at the door. "They called and said they just finished, and they have at least a two-hour drive before they get here. Why don't we sit on the patio and have some wine?"

The evening is cool and there's a slight breeze, so I set my bags in our room, grab a sweater and walk outside. The lilacs are even more beautiful in the evening light; I stop, close my eyes and breathe in their sweet scent. When I hear Eva call my name, I join her on the patio where we both sit in lounge chairs with bright red cushions. Lara emerges from the house carrying a wicker tray that holds three glasses of red wine and a plate of empanadas and sets it on a small wooden table. She sits in the only rocking chair, which creaks as it rocks, and covers her legs with a blanket that, she explains, has been woven by the local Mapuche Indians. I pick up a glass of wine and take a drink. Other than the sound of the rocking chair, the evening is quiet.

"I love it here," says Eva, sipping her wine. "I could stay forever."

I start to answer but hear a truck.

"It's Nico," says Lara, rising from her seat. "He's here to drop off the coolers. I'll be right back." I watch as she walks into the lodge.

"OK," says Eva, "here's your chance; I'm going in. You two behave. Or not."

As Nico walks up the path toward the patio I feel my heart beat faster. His wavy hair is damp and he's wearing jeans, a short-sleeved T-shirt, black vest, and hiking shoes. As he gets closer, I smell cologne.

"Hey, Kate," he says, "how are you doing?" I smile and feel myself blush.

"Good," I tell him. "How are you?"

Before responding, he sits in the rocking chair and takes an empanada off the plate. He eats it in two bites and licks his fingers.

"Good," he replies. "Are you enjoying the evening?" I smile; more small talk.

"Hey," he says, rubbing his hands on his thighs, "I was wondering if you would join me for a horseback ride." I stare at him.

"Sorry?" I ask. "A horseback ride? Now?" He smiles.

"Sure," he replies, "we have time, and it will be fun."

I jump up and set my wine glass on the table.

"Yes, that would be fun, but I have to put on jeans, can you wait?"

"Sure," he says, "better put on a jacket, too."

After changing clothes I walk quickly to the stable and watch as the groom leads our horses into a paddock. I haven't ridden since I was a child in Wyoming, but I try to look confident as Nico helps me into the saddle. After my feet are in the stirrups, I look at him and smile. I can hardly believe my luck that we are spending time alone.

We ride toward the Andes Mountains. At first, our horses walk together before mine trots ahead. When I pull back on the reins, my horse slows down and Nico laughs.

"He likes to be in charge," he says, and I smile.

I suddenly feel too shy to talk to Nico, so I watch my horse as it walks through the dry grass and I rub its neck. Its mane feels like straw and its skin is moist, and I occasionally shift my weight in the creaking saddle to get comfortable. The sun is setting so I look up and see that the sky is the color of amber. I point to it, mouth "pretty" to Nico, and he smiles.

The estancia stretches for miles and miles and dozens of sheep dot the landscape. They run when they see us, bleating their warnings. Nico explains that though they all look alike, the tail lengths are different on males than on females.

"You're opening up a whole new world to me, Nico," I tell him, laughing. "We don't have sheep ranches in Chicago!"

He nods and I watch as he runs his hand through his hair. I imagine that it feels as silky as it looks.

"You want to hear something really interesting?" he asks, stopping his horse. "Look over there."

I turn to see a grove of giant trees near the mountainside and even from here I can see that they're different: tall and stately with clearly delineated branches that reach up toward the sky.

"They're monkey puzzle trees," he says, "nice name, right? They can live for hundreds of years here unless a fire burns them down."

I stare at them for several seconds until Nico moves on. After a few minutes, I ask him about his life in Patagonia.

"It's paradise here," he explains. "The lakes, the rivers, the mountains, they're beautiful. This is my home. It's where I want to be."

It begins to occur to me that my feelings for him are problematic. He lives here and I live in the U.S. He's with Marina and I'm with Andrew. I begin to pull my horse away and swallow hard.

"Rein it in," I tell myself, sadly appreciating the pun, "this wouldn't work."

We ride in silence for several minutes before he suddenly stops. My horse stops alongside.

"Kate, look!" he exclaims, pointing to the sky. "Condors!"

I follow his gaze and see several dark shapes flying near the top of a giant hill. I recognize that they're condors because of what Jason said about their giant wingspans and the white rings around their necks.

"Oh my God," I say as I watch them, "oh my God." Their aerial acrobatics are powerful and mesmerizing as they dive and ascend, then glide, circling one another as if playing. As they soar, my heart soars with them.

"They like to hide," Nico explains, "but it looks like they came out to give you a welcome."

I look at him and blush as he tugs on his horse's reins to get it to walk.

"It's getting late," he says. "We should probably get back." As I guide my horse to follow his, I say, "OK, but promise me that someday we'll do this again."

When we return to the lodge, Andrew and Jason are on the patio. Andrew greets Nico with a handshake and smile.

"Nico," he says, handing me a glass of wine, "how you doin', buddy?" Nico doesn't smile.

"Good," he responds. "How was fishing today?"

I sit on the lounge chair and Andrew sits next to me, draping his arm over my shoulders.

"Great!" he says. "I caught a 20-inch brown. Jason caught one a little larger." Then he turns to me. "You girls shop today?" He hugs me so close that my shoulders hurt.

"Yes," I reply, "we saw Marina and her cousin and a couple of her brothers." I look at Nico, who is staring at the door of the lodge.

"Listen," he says, walking away, "I have to go help Lara. Good to see you."

The next several days we fish with Mike and a guide named Peter. Lara explains that Nico had to take Marina to San Carlos de Bariloche, a three-hour drive, to visit her physical therapist, and that he may not return until after we're gone. I'm surprised and so disappointed that I don't want to fish, and Andrew notices.

"What's wrong, Kate?" he asks. "Tired of fishing?"

I make up an excuse that I'm spending too much time in the sun, so on the last day of fishing I stay at the lodge. Lara serves me lunch outside at a large table that is shaded by towering pine trees; its centerpiece is a loosely woven basket that contains a few pinecones, each the size of a shoe box. When she brings me a large plate that holds a salad and quiche, I say, "*Gracias,*" but push it away. She pauses as if getting ready to say something but shakes her head slightly before returning to the lodge. Sitting there alone I realize that I may never see Nico again, so I get up from my chair, walk slowly among the lilacs and cry. Long rivers of tears stream from my eyes.

The next morning we pack our bags and I head outside to find Eva, only to see Nico, who is helping to load our bags into the trucks. I run over and hug him.

"Kate," he says, hugging me back, "I'll miss being with you. It's been fun helping you to catch fish."

My heart beats faster. He likes to help me catch fish!

"Nico, I'll miss you, too. I'm sorry we couldn't fish together more."

"I'm sorry, too," he says. "I had to take Marina for therapy yesterday, but we'll see each other again. When are you coming back?" I wipe my eyes, sniff and to avoid his gaze, look at the ground and run my shoe along the dirt.

"Kate," he says gently, "you are coming back, aren't you?"

I look up at him and smile.

"I hope to," I tell him, "but it will be a while."

Then he leans over and picks up a small rock. It's brown with pink markings and he brushes it clean with his hands.

"Here," he says, grinning. "You know how much I like to give you rocks. Think of me when you look at it. I want you to come back."

I take the rock from him and smile.

"OK, thank you, Nico. I will."

Then I hear Andrew's voice behind us.

"There you are!" he exclaims. "You about ready to head out?"

I turn to him, nod, tell him I need to say goodbye to Lara, and walk for the last time toward the lodge.

CHAPTER 6
DANCE

We return to Chicago on a Sunday, and I'm eager to get to the newsroom. When Andrew and I walk through our front door, I drop my bags on the floor, tell him I need to meet with Gus and leave. The day is cold and damp and as soon as I walk outside, I begin to sob.

I miss Nico.

I sit on our front steps, bury my face in my hands and cry until my head hurts. I look up only when a young woman approaches. She asks me if I'm all right.

"I'm OK," I tell her, but I'm not. I watch the passersby for several minutes. Each man reminds me of Nico – his stride, his beard and his clothes – but then of course it isn't him, and I cry harder. He is very far away and it's occurring to me that I may never see him again. When I finally walk, I've lost my sense of direction and find myself on a strange street. Eventually I find a taxi, wave it down and tell the driver to take me to the *Tribune* before I sit back, exhausted, and stare out the car's grimy window.

Gus isn't in the newsroom when I arrive, so I walk to my desk and sit down. My computer is off, and next to it is a stack of mail. I know I need to work, but instead I wonder if I can call Argentina. What is the country code? What is Nico's number? Could I send him a text? Would he think it was stupid? Does he Skype? Does he care?

When Gus walks up behind me and removes his jacket, I barely notice and jump when he speaks.

"Kate!" he shouts. "*¡Hola!* Welcome home!" I turn in my chair to look at him, and when he sees me, he steps back.

"Whoa," he says, "are you OK? Something happen to Andrew?"

I shake my head, slump in my chair and stare past him at nothing in particular. He takes off his jacket, pulls a chair next to mine and sits down.

"Kate," he says gently, "I'm serious. What's going on?"

I finally look at him as tears fall down my cheeks.

"I don't know," I tell him. "I'm just very sad."

I tell him about Nico.

"He's handsome, so handsome," I say, "and smart and kind." Gus listens without speaking and watches me closely.

"And," I add, smiling, "you should see him cast a fishing line. It's beautiful, almost magic, really."

I begin to cry again and Gus uses the sleeve of his jacket to wipe my face.

"I don't know what to do," I say, sobbing. "He's so far away."

Gus clears his throat and watches me for several seconds.

"Honey," he finally says, "what do you want to do?"

I look at him and stop crying. His compassion is like a drug and his question is so simple that at first I don't understand.

"What do you mean?" I ask.

"Kate," he says, pulling his chair closer to mine, "I know I'll regret saying this, but there's nothing tying you down here. If you want to be with Nico, why don't you go back?" I don't respond and instead stare at him. How? When? He takes my hand.

"Kate, my dear friend, why don't you just go back?"

Gus stays with me until he can't since we're facing a midnight deadline. After he leaves, I pick up the phone to call Eva who answers after the second ring.

"*¡Hola!*" she shouts into the phone. I pull it away from my ear. "What on earth are you doing at work?"

I say nothing for a second and then begin to cry.

"Eva, I'm going back to Patagonia."

She's silent so I hold my breath, waiting for her to scold me, but instead, she laughs.

"I knew it," she chortles. "I *knew* it! It's Nico, isn't it? Good for you! Go back! And, Katie honey, I'll help you."

After talking with Eva, I search for flights online. I feel drained and tired so I call Andrew to tell him I'm sleeping at my desk.

"Sorry?" he asks, sounding surprised. "At your desk? Why?" I try to think of an excuse.

"I need to catch up," I tell him. "I have hundreds of emails and at least as many notes from Gus. It will make me feel better."

He coughs and clears his throat.

"OK, I understand, but when you want to come home, make

sure that Gus finds you a cab."

When I get home, Andrew sees that I've been crying and he confronts me. We are sitting on opposite ends of our living room couch.

"What's going on?" he asks, his arms crossed at his chest.

I say nothing at first because I don't want to hurt him. I could tell him that he's a good man, a friend, generous to teach me how to fish and take me to Patagonia. I want to tell him that he'll find someone who appreciates him, can tolerate his anger and will be patient with his controlling attitude. I don't want to tell him that I'm not in love with him.

After a few seconds, I try to explain, but my emotions take over.

"I have feelings for Nico," I blurt as I begin to cry. "I'm sorry, Andrew, it just is the way that I feel. I want to go back to Patagonia."

He glares at me, but says nothing until he stands from the couch. His face is red and his eyes are shining and I can't tell if he's about to cry or explode.

"OK," he says angrily before walking away. "But when you pack to leave, make sure you pack to leave for good."

I spend the next several days living with Eva and Jason and decide to return to Patagonia in May. I send an email to Mike asking if I can fish one last time with Nico.

"Sure!" he answers, "and I'll tell him to take you to dinner when you get here!"

Though supportive, Eva wonders if I'm being impetuous.

"First you quickly decide to live with Andrew, and now there's Nico," she cautions one evening while we're setting the table for dinner. "Should I be worried about you?"

I finish pouring water into the glasses before I answer. I try not to sound defensive.

"Eva, I've been living on emotional autopilot for a very long time. When I'm with Nico, I feel a spark of life. It's really that simple."

Andrew has called several times and wants to reconcile, claiming that his bad mood was because he thought he was losing me just like he lost his wife. I tell him that I need time, but I know I need more than that. I need to feel love.

IT'S LATE FALL IN ARGENTINA when I arrive. Though I can't wait to see Nico, I've decided to spend the night in Buenos Aires. I want Lola to teach me how to tango.

As before, she is excited to see me.

"¡Hooolaa!" she cries, running to me as I enter Ezeiza's terminal after customs. This time she's wearing blue jeans and a hooded sweatshirt since it's cold outside.

"The van is parked about a half mile away," she explains as she grabs my bags. "I'll take these, no worries. Give me that one, too. How was your flight?"

I'm so happy to see her that I hug her tight.

"My flight was great," I answer, "I can't believe I'm back

so soon, but I wanted to see San Martín during the off season. *¡Gracias*, Lola!"

"No problem! You know you're staying at the Sofitel and I've arranged for dinner at a tango club and then – are you ready – a milonga!"

Since I don't know what a milonga is, I ask.

"You'll see," she responds, "it's a place where people go to tango, and it's also a style of dance – a bit like tango. You will love it, trust me."

I don't tell Lola the real reason I'm here and she doesn't mention Andrew. As we drive down the highway toward my hotel, I see the city's "shanties" – the country's president has given cinder blocks to the city's residents so they can build their own homes. The cinder blocks are stacked to the level of the highway and are painted in garish bright colors, mostly yellows, reds, greens, and blues. Clotheslines are strung between them like cobwebs where laundry hangs to dry.

"Nice, huh?" asks Lola, periodically checking her phone for messages. "We are not happy about those. Some of the people who live there aren't even Argentines."

After dropping me at my hotel, she takes off with a "Chau, see you at 9!" and I walk to the front desk. For the first time since leaving Chicago, I feel lonely and briefly miss Andrew, but brush away the thought as I check in. When I get to the elevator, the doors open and a couple walk out, holding hands. I lower my head, wonder what Nico is doing and head to my room.

The tango dinner club is in the San Telmo barrio and is crowded when we arrive at midnight. Lola parks at the entrance and the manager allows this since, she assures me, they're very good friends. I'm wearing a long black skirt, red sweater and scarf, but when I pass one of the dancers, I feel overdressed. She's wearing a low-cut dress slit to the top of her thigh, orange tango shoes and fishnets. She's tall and slender and her long dark hair is arranged in a thick braided chignon accessorized with a garish rhinestone comb. Her exaggerated makeup and false eyelashes accentuate her large brown eyes, and her lipstick, like her shoes, is orange. She ignores me, takes her place near the stage and places her hands seductively on her hips. Another dancer approaches, and this time it's a man. He's wearing a white tuxedo and wide-brimmed hat. He stands opposite the woman with his feet spread wide and his arms folded tight.

As Lola and I sit down, the room lights dim and two men walk up a short flight of steps onto the stage. One is carrying a violin, the other an accordion. The piano bench is empty and when the pianist arrives onstage, there is thunderous applause. He bows and sits down as the lights dim. Then the music begins.

Tango originated in the late 1800s along the Río de la Plata, which means River of Silver in Spanish, the natural border between Argentina and Uruguay. There are several styles of tango; in Argentina the dancers embrace and move in perfect unison chest to chest and tonight they do the same. The dancers never smile or speak but communicate through nuance. They watch the floor as they lunge side to side, punctuating their movements with short kicks and hops. Tango is both sensual and erotic. I watch, fascinated, as one dancer presses her back against her partner's chest as he grazes her breasts with his fingertips. Their dance culminates in a near kiss as she slides her hand down his cheek and hugs his leg tight with her thigh.

I am inspired. During intermission I tell Lola that I want to learn to tango. She smiles and nods her head.

"Ah, *sí, sí, sí!* They give lessons upstairs right now. Let's go!" She quickly gestures to our server and I laugh, remembering that she can make anything happen. We run up the steps and at the top, a tall young man greets me with a nod and takes my hand. Silently, he escorts me to a narrow wooden stage lit with red and yellow lights. *Gala Tango* is printed with large gold-leaf letters above it on the wall.

As I take my place on stage I'm met by the same two dancers I saw when we arrived. The woman, now perspiring, appears to be my coach and begins to instruct me in Spanish.

"English, please," I tell her, and she looks at me, but doesn't smile. Her partner, now beside me, takes my hand and places his other hand on the small of my back.

The woman waits until we're ready. She looks annoyed.

"Set your left foot here," she says, jabbing at the stage, "and your right foot there."

The man pulls me close and begins to move as I grip his shoulder. He feels warm and strong, yet I'm unsure of myself and nervous. Sensing this he looks at me, and smiles.

"It's OK," he says, "just follow me," and slowly we begin to dance. Lola applauds.

At 2 a.m. we're back in the car.

"For the milonga we're picking up Mia," Lola announces as we speed through the narrow streets. She leans over my lap, pulls her purse from the floor, reaches in and hands me a slip of paper. "I think I have the address here, will you help?" I take the paper from her hand and read her the address. Ten minutes later we pull to the curb and a petite young woman with short brown hair climbs in the back seat.

"*¡Hola!*" she cries, leaning forward and placing her hand on my shoulder. "I'm Mia! You must be Kate!"

"*¡Sí!*" I respond. "Nice to meet you!"

We drive into Palermo Soho, a barrio known for its fashionable restaurants and nightlife, and Lola parks on a busy street. We walk arm-in-arm down the block; Mia shows me a small cloth bag that she's been carrying inside her large purse. It's cinched at its opening.

"My tango shoes," she explains with a grin. Lola smiles.

"Mia is a tango instructor. She's going to show you how the milonga works."

Three blocks later we enter a building that looks abandoned, but isn't. Inside there's a small video arcade where three teenagers are playing Pac-Man. They turn to us and smile before returning to their game. The floors are stained, and the walls, which badly need painting, are covered with dingy torn posters. On the ceiling there's a large brown water stain the shape of an amoeba. A thin elderly woman wearing a soiled red kerchief sits on a stool at a small ticket counter and smiles at us when we stride by.

"I know that woman," says Lola. "We don't have to pay."

"Of course," I say to Mia, winking, "Lola knows everyone."

We walk down a narrow hall into a large room. On one side there's a bar and on the other, a dance floor. The room is dimly lit except for a tubular neon light that borders the ceiling. The tables are occupied, but the dance floor is empty. I'm disappointed at how dingy things look and wonder why Lola and Mia have brought me here.

As if reading my expression, Mia says, "Follow me," and leads me to the dance floor. Around its periphery are several empty wooden chairs, and we pull three together so Mia can get ready to dance. She unties her cloth bag and carefully removes her shoes; they're white with red high heels and narrow sequined straps. I watch as she puts them on.

"Tango shoes," Lola explains. "You can't wear them on the street. The women put them on here." As Mia buckles her straps, a man approaches. She looks up at him and he nods his head. Without speaking, she stands, takes his hand and they glide to the dance floor.

"Does she know him?" I ask.

"No," explains Lola, "here they dance together first, then they meet."

Fascinated by this concept, I watch as the women leave the bar to sit in the empty chairs. One by one the men approach and lead them to the dance floor. As the couples take their positions, I smile at the myriad differences in style and clothing. One man, short and wearing jeans, dances with a tall woman wearing a low-cut sequined dress; their dance steps, surprisingly, are perfectly in sync. Another couple, both dressed in black, grip one another while trying to figure out their movements, but soon find their rhythm and move closer together. This scene is both sweet and erotic, and I look at Lola. I ache to join them.

"*Sí*," she says, taking my hand, "I know, a lot of passion. You can have this, Kate, you just need to find someone who wants it as much as you."

The next morning Lola takes me to the airport for my flight to Patagonia. After she guides me to security, she leaves me with a hug.

"Safe travels, sweetie," she says. "Enjoy Patagonia! I hope you find peace there – and love."

CHAPTER 7

LEARN

As the plane descends into San Martín de los Andes, I look out the window. On the horizon are the Andes Mountains, and I'm thrilled to once again see Lanín, now covered with snow, as it peeks through the clouds. Below us are the brown rolling hills of Patagonia, each with its unique patchwork of neneos and grass. From this distance it looks as if the hills are draped in brown velvet, and I scan them for wildlife. As the terrain becomes flat, a river is revealed. It's long, winding and blue and I'm flooded with memories of fishing with Nico.

Before leaving the U.S. I read countless books about Patagonia. The region, which spans more than 400,000 square miles, includes glaciers, mountains, lakes, and rivers, enticing adventurers to explore. Today I am no different. I want to experience Patagonia without Andrew's itinerary.

When we land at Chapelco Airport, the passengers applaud and I happily join them, but I hesitate to rise from my seat. Nico will pick me up from my hotel for dinner, but how will he react? Will he be happy to see me, or will he be married to Marina? I resolve that it's too late to turn back, so I pull my backpack from the overhead and button my sweater. I slowly step down the metal staircase to the tarmac as a gentle wind blows through my hair. I sense that winter is approaching because I feel cool air on my face. The azure sky is partly cloudy, and other than sounds from the plane, the area is quiet.

Unlike Ezeiza in Buenos Aires, where buses transport arriving passengers to a variety of terminals, there is only one terminal here, and it's small. I walk inside and stand near the only conveyor belt to wait for my bags. Suddenly, I hear a dog bark. Where? I wonder. Then I see a young man as he runs into the room and gently pushes his way through the crowd. He's wearing cargo pants, a sweatshirt and sneakers, and when he gets to the conveyor belt, he grabs a small dog crate that's sitting among the arriving luggage. Holding it high to move quickly through the crowd, he runs back out. I gather my bags and walk outside just in time to see him unlatch the crate in the parking lot. An exuberant puppy, black with white paws, runs out, and the man kneels to pick it up. He embraces the puppy as it licks his face and when he puts it down, it runs around in circles, happily barking. The man claps his hands and laughs, and the puppy snuggles against his legs. Their reunion is sweet and I smile. Only a few more hours, I think, until I see Nico.

A small taxi picks me up for the 20-minute ride to town and I roll down the window to enjoy the fresh air. The sudden rush of wind whips my hair into my face and I quickly brush it from my eyes. The scent of pine fills the car and I search the hills for monkey puzzle trees, remembering what Nico taught me. It's late autumn here, and the deciduous trees have orange, red and gold leaves. White mist hovers along the tree lines. In contrast, the ground is dry and sparsely covered with various wheat-colored grasses. As I scan the area for mementos of my previous visit, we pass a gaucho riding on a horse near the roadside. The taxi driver beeps a greeting and I wave out the window. The gaucho turns his head and waves back.

Further along there's a soccer field with a black dirt surface. Soccer is a major sport in Argentina and often ignites passionate debate when the country plays against Brazil. Today it looks like simple fun, with dozens of spectators cheering and blowing horns as a young boy scores a goal. Their exuberance is infectious and I cheer softly as we drive by.

As we enter San Martín de los Andes I feel like a high school girl with a crush. Will I see Nico as we drive through town? And if I do, will I slump down in the seat to hide? My adrenalin is rushing and suddenly I feel vulnerable. What will happen during this trip? Will I be welcomed or rejected? Will I leave happy or sad? Or will I leave at all?

Unlike during its peak seasons, when its streets and plazas are full of tourists, San Martín is quiet in May. Most of the shops are closed until ski season, which begins in July. As we drive down Avenue San Martín, the town's main street, I look out my window and feel privileged to witness this transformation from bustling resort town to residential community. At the same time I feel shy and respectful. I don't want to intrude.

My *hostería*, the Plaza Mayor, is at the top of a small hill at the end of a narrow street that's lined with small one-story houses and restaurants. The *hostería* itself is tucked against a hill and resembles a Swiss chalet with its peaked roof, decorative woodwork and large shiny windows. The taxi driver pulls into the driveway and opens the trunk to unload my bags. I walk to the front door and see that there's a doorbell. "Quaint," I think, as I press it with my finger. I hear the chimes inside and a middle-aged woman, attractive and petite, opens the door.

"*¡Buenas tardes!*" she says cheerfully as she reaches out to shake my hand. "Welcome! You must be Kate. We've been expecting you!"

A man appears behind her to take my bags from the driver and he smiles at me. The woman's name is Mecha, short for Mercedes, and she's lovely. Her big smile and enthusiastic welcome warm my heart and I want to know more about her. I move into the lobby and look around. The front desk is small and the dining area is ahead. To the left is a separate room with a fireplace, plush couches, chairs, and tables lined with various knickknacks, including a small metal box with a stamped design and stone sculpture of a reclining woman. On the walls are Dutch plates hung in various patterns, separated by an occasional watercolor print. I immediately feel at home and am pleased to be in this comfortable place.

Mecha walks me to my room, which is small but suitable. It

has a queen-sized bed with a white spread, two side tables and a vanity. The windows are large and I immediately pull them open. The view is breathtaking; the mountains, full of towering pine trees, loom in the distance and I hear distant screaming birds. I imagine that they're caracaras, Argentina's well-known birds of prey, which I read about before this trip. The air is cool, and light mist begins to fill the room.

Since it's early I change clothes and walk to town. Most of the houses are constructed of stone and wood, and I am delighted to see that in one yard there are a dozen red and white rosebushes still in bloom. In the street, two young boys wearing shorts and sweatshirts kick a soccer ball back and forth. One accidentally kicks the other and I wince as the injured boy begins to cry. I ask him if I can help, but he briskly shakes his head and runs away.

I choose to walk in the quiet street instead of on the sidewalks, which are broken to the dirt in several places. Soon, a dirty golden lab, black terrier and brown dachshund join me, happily trotting together in near-perfect unison. They appear to be the best of friends. The dachshund is trying hard to keep up. They follow me for a block before turning at the corner, and soon disappear into a nearby yard.

As I walk down the street I watch the cars drive by. I see a pickup truck and imagine it's a fishing guide, and can't help but smile. Suddenly, I feel a wave of intense pleasure that begins at my throat and travels to my toes. I stop, my cheeks burn and my entire body tingles as if all of my cells, once dormant, have suddenly and simultaneously come alive. The sensation feels new and I'm surprised by its swiftness and power.

"What is this?" I wonder, and remember that it's the same tingling I felt when I first touched Nico's hand. Elated, I laugh out loud. Only a few hours more before I see him.

Because it's getting cooler, I zip my jacket and reach into my pockets to pull out my black leather gloves. As I put them on I remember that Andrew gave them to me for Christmas. Though grateful, I quickly tuck the memory away and continue to walk.

The street ends at Avenue San Martín. I look to my left then to my right and see no one. I'm alone for now and eager to explore. Most of the shops are closed, but their wares are strategically placed near the entrances to entice street shoppers. I walk slowly and see that the first shop sells toys. The shop's window is full of brightly colored dolls, books, miniature cars, and superheroes that are similar to those in the U.S. This is both whimsical and enticing and I press my hands against my cheeks and laugh. Children everywhere, I think, love the same toys! Strolling farther I see a woman's clothing store, eyeglass shop, music store, and pharmacy. A bookstore has the same titles that I've read, except they're in Spanish.

I want to cross the street and stop at the curb to wait for two passing cars. A bus pulls up a few yards away, stops and opens its door to pick up a woman carrying two large shopping bags. A scruffy brown dog, no larger than a cat, runs up to climb in behind her. The dog appears to be a stray and I watch sadly as it tries hard to reach the bottom step and is shooed away by the driver who then closes the door. The dog watches the bus as it drives away, so I walk over, pick it up and scratch its head. It licks my cheek at first, but then wiggles to get away. I set it gently on the sidewalk and watch as it runs down the sidewalk.

On the other side of the street there is a souvenir shop and since it's open, I walk inside. A tiny bell rings to indicate my arrival. The shop is full of Patagonia memorabilia, including gaucho knives, maté gourds, bombillas, and beer steins that say, *San Martín de los Andes*. Dozens of refrigerator magnets hang on the walls with miniature pictures of Chapelco Ski Resort, located outside of town, the Andes Mountains, condors, and smiling fly-fishermen catching leaping trout. On the glass counter are stacks of wooden bowls and plates crafted by the local Mapuche Indians. The manager is a man who speaks with a German accent. When he asks if he can help me I say, "No thank you" and leave. The garishness has disturbed me since this is not the Patagonia that I have grown to love.

On the next corner is a store named Spirit Patagonia. A perfect name, I think, as I peer inside. It sells sporting goods for skiing, biking and *fútbol* and its windows are full of colorful parkas, backpacks, ski gloves, and goggles. It's also open and I peer through the window just in time to see a tall young man kneel to greet a young girl who has just entered the store with an attractive young couple. She wears a hooded yellow parka and her long blonde hair is pulled into a ponytail wrapped with a bright green scrunchie.

"*¡Hoooolaaa!*" exclaims the man, arms outstretched. He picks her up, hugs her tight and plants an exaggerated kiss on her cheek. I savor this moment for a few seconds and leave.

At the end of the avenue I hear a motorbike as it roars down the street. I look to find it and watch, fascinated, as the driver, dressed in tight blue jeans and black jacket, steers it onto the sidewalk and stops in front of a small pizza restaurant. After setting the kickstand with his foot, he swings his leg over the seat and strides briskly inside, still wearing his helmet and dark face shield. His machismo is both striking and appealing. Motorbikes are common here and adventuresome young men ride them everywhere, even in rough mountainous terrain. It's risky to navigate Patagonia's rugged landscape, so men who have grown up here, including Nico, are strong, smart and capable.

Since I haven't eaten since breakfast, I stop in a small diner to eat lunch. Most of the few tables are occupied, but I find a small two-top in the corner. I sit quietly, wanting to be inconspicuous, but nearly everyone looks at me.

"New kid in town," I think.

I'm distressed but not surprised that the menu is in Spanish, and since the waitress speaks little English, I order what I recognize, which is a chicken Caesar salad. The salad is simple and delicious, but because I feel out of place I eat quickly. Before the waitress can give me a ticket, I put 80 pesos on the table, more than enough, and quickly walk out the door to return to the hotel.

As I walk down the streets of San Martín, I fantasize about

Nico. How would I describe him to my father if he were still alive? I imagine that I would write him a letter from my room at the *hostería*. I would write it as a journalist.

"Dad," I would write, "I think I'm in love. His name is Nico, and he lives here. He's intelligent and resourceful, is socially and culturally sophisticated and is friendly with most of the town's residents who like and respect him for his work ethic and guiding skills. He moves easily in sync with Patagonia's rhythm and beauty, is strong and athletic, deftly navigates its rivers and lakes, and enjoys riding his motorbike along its steep mountain trails. He quickly mastered the area's ski slopes and as a young man would ride his bicycle into the hills so he could jump from the cliffs into the nearby lakes. He chooses to live in those same hills because it relaxes his soul. Mostly, he's nice to me, Dad. I know you will learn to love him as I do."

When I get to my room, I nap. The windows are still open and the fresh air is soothing. I hear church bells in the distance and Mecha's muffled voice as she speaks to the *hostería* staff in Spanish. Drifting to sleep I commit to learning the language yet dream of home. Though Patagonia is my resting place, I wonder if I could live here forever, surrounded by mountains and sheltered from the outside world.

The hotel's front door is unlocked in the evenings to accommodate guests who dine in town. Thus, when I'm to see Nico, I wait alone in the lobby. I wear a black wool dress, blue sweater and boots, and though the night is cold, I'm too warm to bring a coat. I sit on a bench near the door and periodically check my watch; he's scheduled to arrive at 9:30 since our dinner reservations are at 10. Argentines, like Europeans, dine late, and it's not uncommon to stay out until the early morning hours. When I hear the crunch of gravel, I know he's arrived so I stand and smooth my dress. My lips feel dry and my heart beats fast. I've waited for this moment for a very long time and now that it's here, I can barely contain my excitement. I try to remain calm.

When Nico walks through the door I giggle. He is as I remember him: rugged and beautiful with dark wavy hair and kind green eyes. His soft beard is trimmed and he wears a black hooded jacket, blue jeans and gray down vest. When he smiles and opens his arms, I run to him, eager for his hug. Our embrace is tight; he feels warm and strong and I don't want to let him go. Instead, I press my cheek against his shoulder, which feels like a soft silk pillow.

"Kate," he says softly in his deep, mellow voice. "How are you?"

I look at him and smile. How am I? My throat is tight and I cannot speak. My body feels weightless and my knees are shaking. I've longed for Nico for so many weeks and here he is, by my side. I want to tell him I've lived only for this moment, but instead I say, "I'm fine!" And as I stand here with the man I want to wake to each morning, I know, without a doubt, that I am in love.

Dinner is at La Tasca, a popular restaurant that's full during tourist season but empty tonight. It's warm and inviting with eclectic décor and dozens of tables adorned with red and white tablecloths. As Nico speaks to the maître d', I scan the room; the back wall is lined with large wooden barrels and dozens of wine bottles. On the front wall above the picture window there is a large print of the Three Stooges wearing golf attire. *Golf with your friends*! it says, and I laugh; even the Argentines appreciate Stooges humor. There's another print of Louis Armstrong playing his trumpet with his cheeks puffed out like pillows. A ledge near the window holds two tall plants and I am pleased to see that they're real. As Nico and I sit down, a server approaches with two menus. She's tall and strikingly beautiful; her black hair is pulled tight into a bun near the top of her head and her soft straight bangs end just above her eyebrows. Her lipstick is bright red. She greets us in crisp, accented English and asks what we want to drink. Nico glances up from the menu.

"Malbec?" he asks, and I nod.

We both order smoked deer, fries and a salad. When the server leaves I cross my hands in my lap and lean forward.

"I can't believe I'm here," I say to him, then immediately regret it, since I know how he'll respond.

"Yes and why *are* you here? Fishing season is nearly over." Then he smiles before continuing. "I'm glad you're here, Kate, it must be the rock that I gave you. It brought you back."

I blush and smile.

"It's not great fishing now," he continues, "but we might catch a few. Did you bring your gear?"

I watch the server as she delivers our food.

"Yes," I answer, "I brought my waders and boots and a 6-weight rod."

"Great," he says, before popping a French fry into his mouth, "we can go to the Chimehuin. It is possible that there will be some fish there, we'll see."

CHAPTER 8

LOVE

Nico picks me up before dawn and loads my gear into his truck. It's cold and damp and the headlights illuminate the mist. I see the blue cooler – our blue cooler – behind the back seat and ask him if he'd made lunch. "Yes," he replies with a grin. "I brought your favorite olives." I think, "Ah-love olives." He remembered. He opens the passenger door, I climb inside and he hands me the seat belt.

"I want you to be safe," he says as I click it into place.

Then he shuts the door, walks to the driver's side and climbs inside. I watch as he does this and feel happy to be alive. He closes his door and turns to me.

"I'm glad you're here, Kate," he says as he shifts the truck into gear. "We'll go to the river soon, but first I want to show you something."

We drive through town and head into the mountains. We're silent until he pulls to the side of the road and then he tells me to wait and runs to my door to open it. He takes my hand and leads me to the railing at the side of the road.

I look down; the hills below are dotted with hundreds of

tiny bright lights. It's the town, asleep, its street lamps aglow. In the distance I see a lake, its surface shimmering in the fading moonlight, and the gray light of dawn on the horizon.

"It's so beautiful," I whisper. Nico leans close and points to the lake. His hair smells like mint shampoo.

"Yes," he says, "look over there. It's Lácar Lake. I like this time of day and I wanted you to see it." Then he squeezes my hand.

When we arrive at the river the sun is rising. Nico parks near the riverbank and readies the boat. He takes my hand to help me climb in and spends a few minutes rigging my rod.

"OK," he says, handing it to me, "cast on the left." As he rows I pull the fly loose, cast the line and immediately hook a trout.

"Nice!" he says, releasing the anchor. I pull the fish to the boat and he scoops it into the net. "A nice rainbow," he says proudly as he unhooks the fish. He gently releases it to the water. He sits down, pulls the anchor up and begins to row. I look around and hear Patagonia as it awakens: birds chirping in the trees, a muskrat splashing nearby. I smile at Nico and he smiles back.

"What are you looking at?" he asks.

"You, guiding," I tell him.

"That's what I do," he responds, "and you fish." I wait for a moment before speaking again.

"What if you fish?" I finally ask. He smiles again, then points to the water.

"Look," he says, "a rise."

I glance at the water and the surface is smooth. I know he's changing the subject.

"Seriously, Nico, you could fish for a while. I would like to watch you cast again."

He stops rowing.

"OK," he says as he releases the anchor. He takes my rod and stands as he pulls line from the reel. He raises his hand, jerks the rod back and the line makes a perfect loop. When he jerks the rod forward the line shoots toward the shoreline and lands gently on the water. The fly floats upright in the distance as if it landed there by itself, and I clap my hands with delight. At this moment, life is perfect. The respect and love I feel for Nico are unlike anything I've experienced before. What is it about him that tugs at my heart? What is it about *us*?

We stop for lunch at noon. The sky is clear and the air is cool so I put on my blue fleece jacket. Nico steers the boat to the tree-lined bank and jumps out to pull it onto the gravel. I climb out and walk up a hill that's shaded by a thick grove of willows. The ground is covered with tiny rocks and uneven patches of grass. I watch Nico as he pulls two folded chairs and a table from our boat, sets them on the ground and returns to the boat for the cooler. I look around and see a small white house in the distance and wonder if anyone lives there. Then I hear a splash and turn to see a kingfisher flying up to a low branch over the water. It looks around, flattens its wings against its body and dives in again, this time retrieving a tiny wriggling fish. As it returns to the branch with the fish in its mouth, I clap my hands and watch Nico as he assembles the table and covers it with a green striped tablecloth. On it he places two wooden plates, a small fish-shaped platter and two paper napkins.

"Hungry?" he asks as he opens the cooler and begins removing the food.

"Yes," I say, "starving. And you?"

"Yes," he says, pulling off lids and returning them to the cooler, "starving."

Lunch is fried chicken, cheese and a pasta salad mixed with red peppers and onions. He passes me a covered container; inside are several green olives.

"¡*Gracias!*" I tell him.

Then he opens a bottle of Malbec and pours it into two metal cups that are shaped like hourglasses. We touch the cups together, say, "Cheers!" and drink. The wine is sweet and mellow and as I swallow it I feel warm.

The chicken and pasta salad are delicious and we eat it all. Dessert is chocolate pudding that we enjoy with instant coffee. When we finish I rise from my chair and walk to the cooler to place the empty containers inside. Soon, I feel Nico beside me.

"Kate," he says softly, and I turn to look. Without speaking, he places his hands gently on my cheeks and kisses me softly on my lips.

"At last," I think, my legs feeling weak, "this is it."

I wrap my arms around his neck and kiss him back. His mouth tastes sweet and he feels strong as he pulls me close. We kiss for a very long time before he pulls away, takes my hand and leads me to a dirt trail that winds in and out of the trees. We walk in silence for several minutes. My senses are acute. I feel the long grass as it brushes against my legs, see insects running from the trail and hear a woodpecker tapping in the distance. Nico's palm feels moist and we tighten our grip as we finally reach a clearing.

"Kate," he says, pulling me close, "I hope you don't mind." I look ahead and see with delight that we're headed for the small white house.

As it turns out, the house is Nico's. After we enter he leads me to the bedroom and we eagerly undress. Now naked, we pause, look at each other and smile. When we embrace, I feel his excitement as I gently stroke his back; his skin feels warm and soft. He touches me with such tenderness that it makes me cry, so he stops, wipes away my tears and leads me to the bed. After we lie down, he covers me with the sheet and pulls me close. I've dreamt of this moment, wondering how he would feel, so I turn to him, lay my palm on his cheek, and lightly trace his beard with my fingertips. When I reach his lips, he kisses my hand and my body tingles from my head to my toes. I pull down the sheet, press my body against his and then we make love – hungrily, eagerly, happily – until the sun begins to set in the magnificent Patagonia sky.

Afterward, our bodies intertwined, I watch Nico as he sleeps. His breathing is deep and rhythmic and I smile, remembering the first moment I saw him. His green eyes, so expressive and kind, are now closed. His long dark lashes are spread evenly above his cheekbones. His wavy hair, thick and silky, lies haphazardly around his head atop the worn white pillowcase. I lightly touch his chest and feel his heart beat; his skin, lighter in color than his suntanned arms, feels moist. I'm so enamored, so besotted by this wonderful man that I want him to know, so I rub his stomach until he awakens, kiss him everywhere from his ankles to his waist and linger where it makes him happiest. After his orgasm I kiss his mouth, slowly and deeply, while he caresses my back. When he wraps his arms around me and I snuggle against his chest, he speaks. His voice vibrates to my soul.

"Kate, I missed you." A tear seeps from my eye.

When we dress to leave, Nico tells me about the house. He explains that he stays there early in the fishing season to see which insects the fish are eating, and he ties flies that mimic them. Though I respect his guiding abilities, I suddenly feel shy and don't know what to say. I think of something neutral, something safe.

"Seriously!" I cry. "Now that's amazing!"

Because we've made love, the space between us has changed and we now face issues that need to be resolved. But instead of thinking about Andrew, Marina, responsibilities, or consequences, I sit on the edge of the bed and pull on my boots as if nothing has happened at all.

Nico, already dressed, sits beside me.

"Kate," he says, "I want you to stay. I don't want you to leave, to go back to Chicago."

I take his hand.

"I know," I tell him, "I don't want to leave. But how can I stay? Marina loves you, I don't have a job here and you hate the city. How?"

Nico stands from the bed and walks to the door.

"I know those things and we have to figure it out. This is where I live. This is what I love. But I also love you."

I look at him for a moment and then begin to sob, my body quaking, tears pouring onto my lap. He rushes over, pulls me up, wraps his arms around me, and holds me tight. His strength calms me, but I feel ashamed, exposed and confused. This is my watershed moment and I know it. I can never go back.

"I love you, too, Nico," I cry. "I love you, too."

After several minutes he whispers softly in my ear.

"Kate, it will be OK, but we have to leave. It's getting dark."

The sun has set by the time we arrive at the river's take-out point. I feel drained and tired and Nico is silent as he rushes the boat onto the trailer and packs our gear into the truck. I sit on the trunk of a tree that was long ago downed by the river's overflow and remove my boots and waders, trying not to wonder what will happen when we get back to town. Will we stay together in my *hostería* or will he invite me to his house? Will he just drop me off or whisk me away to a mountain chalet to toast our new relationship? Or – and I struggle not to think of this – will he want to be with Marina? I choose not to ask "What now?" and he doesn't offer, until we're inside the truck.

"Dinner?" he asks, turning to me. I look at him and feel relieved. This is a new relationship, delicate, with undertones of guardedness. I know that my heart can be shattered in an instant, but I say yes. I look at Nico and fall in love all over again. His beautiful eyes sparkle in the dusky light and his gaze is tender, loving and inviting. I want to hold and protect him, give him everything I have plus the sun, moon and stars. I've already left Andrew, my job and my previous life. I had given no thought to how reckless this was, how much pain I caused or whether Nico even cared. At this moment I don't want the day to end and watch Nico as he takes my hand and gently kisses my palm. Then I put my hand on his thigh and kiss him on the mouth.

"I would like that," I say as I pull away. "Where?"

"My place," he answers, turning the key in the ignition. "You might as well see where I live."

Nico's home is at the top of a hill. Though he mentioned it before, I didn't realize it was nearly a mile from town. We drive for several minutes on a rutted dirt road before I see the house. At first I wonder if it's a library or school because it's so large. Constructed of wood and stone and modern in design, it has giant picture windows and a peaked metal roof dotted with several large skylights. We pull into the driveway and Nico turns off the engine. A porch light is on and a dog barks inside.

"Anabel," he explains as we climb from the truck. "She's friendly, almost too friendly. I hope you like her."

Indeed, Anabel is friendly. When Nico opens the door and switches on the light, she jumps on me and licks my hands. A petite border collie, she dashes out the back door as soon as it's opened and barks at the sky with abandon. She reminds me of the dogs in town and I smile as I unzip my jacket. Freedom, I think. It's so underrated.

Nico's home is a masterpiece. It has several overstuffed couches and chairs, a dining room with seating for 18 people and a large eat-in kitchen. The walls are covered with various works of art: gauchos riding through the Andes by the famous Patagonia painter, Georg Miciu, and photos of fly-fishing by Georg's equally talented son, Isaias Miciu Nicolaevici. The kitchen's walls are lined with shelves painted in bright pastel colors and many hold maté gourds of various designs and sizes. Argentines greatly value social interaction and it's common for friends to stop by without notice to share maté and conversation. It's one of the traditions I love most about Patagonia.

"I don't have much to eat," says Nico as he helps me remove my jacket. "Are you hungry?" I think about it for a second and say no. I sit on one of the couches, remove my shoes and pat the seat to invite him to sit with me. When he does, he removes his jacket and boots and takes my hand. We sit in silence for several seconds before he pulls me to him and wraps his arm around my shoulders.

"Kate," he says softly, "I'm still with Marina."

I feel my body get tense. "I figured as much," I say, pulling away, "and that's OK. Are you happy?"

"We have our problems," he says as he stretches his arm on the back of the couch. "We've been together a long time and we work them out. I don't want to hurt her."

I am confused. Why is he with me? I say nothing for several seconds before I place my hands next to my thighs, lift myself up and move away.

"Does she know I'm here?" I ask.

He's silent for a moment, then cups his hand to his mouth and coughs slightly before responding.

"No," he says, finally.

It's interesting how matters of the heart can warp reality. After Nico mentions Marina, I think of Andrew. Having pushed him from my mind, he now looms as if he's in the next room. I want him to leave, to walk down the dirt road and disappear into the evening mist, but he doesn't. Instead, he stands there with his shoulders slumped, arms hanging at his sides. I see the hurt in his eyes as he asks silently, "How could you?" But instead of getting up and embracing him, instead of saying, "I'm sorry," I sit there and close my eyes. This is my fantasy, I think stubbornly; please don't control this, too. I love Nico and he loves me. How wrong can this possibly be?

I open my eyes and look at Nico and defiantly stand up. I kneel on the couch and then sit, facing him, on his lap. He puts his hands on my hips as I kiss his mouth with almost desperate fervor. I stop and stroke his soft, smooth beard and kiss him again, this time gently, as I run my fingers through his silky hair. As I feel him rise beneath me, I pull off my shirt and then his before he stands with me in his lap. As he carries me to the bedroom I wrap my legs around his waist and snuggle my face against his neck. His scent is erotic – a blend of musk and desire – so I say, "I want you so much" before he gently sets me on his bed. Lying back, I close my eyes and hear Anabel barking in the distance. As Nico removes my clothes I think to myself, "May this day never end" and arch my back as he kisses my breasts. I definitely, most definitely, am in love with this man.

Afterward we sleep. When Nico wakes up, he pulls on a pair of shorts and tells me to stay in bed.

"I'm going to cook you a steak," he announces. The room is dark and I listen as he moves around the kitchen; at one point I squeal happily into the pillow since I can hardly believe I'm here.

When the steak is ready, he returns to the bedroom, reaches into his closet, pulls out a T-shirt, and tosses it to me.

"This is for you," he says.

I put it on, walk barefoot into the kitchen and help him make a salad of lettuce, carrots and radishes.

We sit across from each other at the dining room table with our feet touching, two worn candles burning slowly between us. We eat voraciously and finish every bite, then share a bowl of *dulce de leche* ice cream for dessert. We talk about nothing important and since I'm tired, this is a huge relief. We return to bed without washing the dishes and sleep soundly, only waking once to make love again.

The next morning I hear my phone beeping with text messages. I think I'm dreaming until I awaken and see Nico. He's still asleep and facing me with his head buried in an overstuffed pillow. I pull the sheet to his shoulders and get up, stepping over Anabel as I walk to the living room to retrieve my phone.

The messages are from Gus, and he's relentless.

"Got to call me, impt, where the f are you?" says the text. Then another: "Wtg, seriously, call now, ned your pword to get doc re asment, cant find it on dktop, called, yr vmail is full!! What the f??"

I move to the kitchen and text him back.

"Gus, I'm the f?? in Ptgonia, only 800 here, will call later, sent doc via email to u 2 days ago pls chk let me know."

I turn off the phone, lay it on the kitchen table and then tiptoe to the bathroom. The house is quiet and the early morning light shines through the stained glass, casting a rainbow of color on the floor. I look outside and see a grove of pine trees that are brightly lit by the sun as it rises in the distance. Dew glistens on the grass and I watch as a small brown bird pulls a worm from the dirt and swallows it whole.

In my reverie I think of my father and what he said to me when I was five. We were walking together at our vacation house and I was pushing my toy stroller. Inside the stroller was my precious doll, Pink Lace, named after her dress, and we came to a mountain of steps that led to our front door. It was time for dinner, getting dark, and I didn't want to leave Pink Lace outside. After considering my options, I picked up the stroller to carry it up the steps. It was heavy and my father stood next to me watching as I carried it up one step and then two.

"Kate baby," he said softly, "there is a better way."

I stopped, out of breath, looked up, and saw that he was smiling. "What?" I asked.

"Take Pink Lace out of her stroller and carry her inside. You can leave the stroller here."

I thought about it for a second.

"No!" I was defiant. "She likes to sleep in here, Daddy!"

He reached down, picked me up and kissed me on the cheek. I began to cry.

"Kate baby," he said, "you're strong, but not strong enough to carry that stroller. Sometimes you have to make decisions that you don't like. Right now what is best for her may not be best for you."

I began to sob and he stroked my hair.

"I am strong, Daddy! I am strong!" I buried my face in his shoulder.

"Don't cry, baby," he said, scooping Pink Lace from the stroller and carrying us both up the steps. "Everything will be all right. I promise that everything will be all right."

Now, years later, I'm in Patagonia and everything is not all right. I'm in love with a man who's devoted to another and Andrew is at home, hurting. Like my father told me when I was five, I have to figure out what is best for me. But do I know what that is? Though I've never felt happier, I'm perched on a mountain of doubt. Can I stay here? Should I return home? Feeling suddenly cold, I decide to think about these things later and walk back to the bedroom to be with Nico.

CHAPTER 9
SET

When I return to bed, I roll onto my side with my back to Nico and snuggle into his chest. He wraps his arms around me and I pull them close, folding his hands into mine. He kisses the back of my neck as Anabel jumps onto the bed, licks our faces and barks.

"I got this," he says, standing up. "She needs to go outside." I watch as he pulls on his shorts to follow Anabel to the back door. Left alone, I scan the room to see what's there: a high-back wooden chair and two end tables, each with a tall narrow lamp; a large antique dresser with Nico's personal items on top – his keys, phone, wallet, and a half-empty bottle of water. On the wall, which is painted white, there are three colorful framed prints, which I recognize as Picasso's "Mediterranean Landscape," Van Gogh's "Café" and Benito Quinquela Martín's "La Boca de Quinquela." A flash of color catches my eye and I look to my right. I am saddened, but not surprised, to see a woman's pink robe, hanging from an ornate brass hook on the front of the closet door.

Before I left Chicago, Eva told me to be careful. "I support you going back to Argentina," she said, munching on a salad during lunch at Nordstrom, "but you know that Nico's involved with Marina. This will not end well." I refused to agree.

"I don't care," I declared as I sipped the last of my iced tea through a tall narrow straw. "There's something there and I need to know what it is." Eva shook her head.

"I understand you care about him but I don't want you to get hurt. His life is there and your life is here. And Marina's family and friends will hate you. Plus, being with an Argentine man is every woman's dream. What if he cheats on you like he did with Marina?"

I felt my cheeks burn as I opened my purse to pay the bill, which was lying on a small tray along with two chocolate-covered thin mints wrapped in foil. I wanted to end the discussion.

"Thank you," I said, "but I really think I'm in love with him. I want to feel that, to finally understand what that means. I think he feels the same about me."

Eva wiped her mouth with her napkin, folded it neatly and placed it next to her plate on the table. Then she leaned close and spoke to me in her most soothing voice.

"Katie honey, I know, and I hate to sound like Dr. Phil, but the best love you can hope for is the love you give yourself."

As Nico walks into the bedroom, I swing my legs over the side of the bed. I tell him I want to go for a walk. He looks at me, puzzled.

"OK," he yawns, stretching his arms over his head. "Now?"

"Yes," I reply as I stand and face him, covering myself with a large corner of the sheet. "It's beautiful outside. Morning is my favorite time of day."

We shower together. I wash his hair before he washes mine and I spray him with water after he squirts me with soap. After we dress, I walk to the kitchen to find coffee. I'm wearing the same cargo pants from the day before and Nico's T-shirt; on the front is a multicolored trout with the word *Pesca!* (Fish) below in bright orange letters. As I stand there I try to be calm, but having seen the woman's robe, I want to hide. Grabbing my fishing cap from the counter, I put it on, pulling my wet hair into a ponytail and shoving it through the back opening. I tug the visor over my eyes.

When Nico walks into the kitchen he pulls a bag of coffee and French press from a tall white cabinet and sets them on the counter. He fills a bright red teapot with hot water and begins to heat it on the stove before pulling a bag of croissants from a breadbasket. I watch as he packs breakfast for our hike: four of the croissants, two large chunks of Manchego cheese, a bunch of green grapes, and two giant red apples. He scoops generous spoonfuls of coffee into the French press and pours the boiling water on top. After pressing it down, he drains the coffee into a small brown thermos, tightens the lid and places everything into a green North

Face backpack that has orange piping around its edges. Only then does he stop to look at me. His dark curls and beard are still damp from the shower and he's wearing baggy blue jeans and a faded blue T-shirt with a black condor, wings extended, printed on the front. His feet, brown from the sun, are bare.

"You're so beautiful, Kate," he says, smiling, his voice catching slightly, "so beautiful."

I tear off my cap, run to him and throw my arms around his neck.

"You are too!" I cry, kissing him. "You are too!"

Our hike starts at the back of the house with Anabel tagging along. It's still cool, and we walk side by side holding hands until the trail narrows at the base of a hill. Birds squawk all around us, and at one point a caracara runs ahead of us on the trail. It has bright orange legs.

"Someone needs to tell him that he can fly," laughs Nico.

Every few minutes I touch the back of his jacket to reassure myself that we're together. I don't know how long this will last but I decide that I will enjoy the day and not make an issue of Marina.

An hour into our hike we stop to eat breakfast. We sit on a fallen log and pull our food from the backpack as Anabel hunts nearby. When she sees movement beneath the fallen pine needles, she freezes before chasing an invisible force along the forest floor.

"Probably a mouse," explains Nico, as he pours coffee into the thermos' metal cup for us to share. He hands me a croissant; I peel it apart, handing him a large buttery layer.

"*Gracias*," he says before popping it into his mouth.

I watch as he carefully slices the cheese and apples with a pocketknife and arranges them on his jacket.

"I forgot to bring a plate," he says, shyly. "We can eat from here."

My eyes fill with tears. He's such a gentle soul. We chat about the forest and fishing, and then he tells me about the ski resort. It's only a mile away. I ask if I can see it.

"Sure," he says as he tucks the remains of our breakfast into the backpack, "I'll take you tomorrow. There's not much there but you'll like the view."

We get back to the house at noon and I see a compact car parked behind Nico's truck. I stop, concerned, as Nico keeps walking. When he notices that I'm not following him, he turns around.

"It's OK, Kate," he says. "It's only Felipe. He's here to pick up the lamb from the freezer for tonight's *asado.*"

Felipe waves to me as Nico leads him to the garage. I head for the bedroom, take off Nico's T-shirt, fold it, and place it on the bed. Trying not to look at the woman's robe, I put on my fishing shirt, tuck my hair inside my cap and walk outside.

After Felipe leaves, Nico drives me to Plaza Mayor. When we reach town, he tells me he'll take me to dinner tomorrow night. I feel my throat tighten and look at him, surprised, suddenly understanding that I won't be going to the *asado.* He doesn't look at me and instead, drives in silence. When I say nothing, he pulls to the side of the road and stops.

"Kate, Marina will be there tonight," he says. "We planned this many months ago." I look down at my lap. Here we go, I think, complications of our relationship.

"I don't know what else to say, Kate," he continues, taking my hand. "I can't let her down. It's her birthday." I look at him, swallow hard and smile.

"It's OK, Nico, I understand. Just take me back to the *hostería*." After he smiles at me and continues to drive, I decide to return to Chicago as quickly as I can. This, I admit silently to Eva, is me being impetuous.

MECHA TELLS ME I can't get a flight to Buenos Aires for three days. Not knowing what else to do, I hike along Lácar Lake. The exercise calms me and I try to focus on the area's beauty. The sky is clear and bright and the lake shimmers in the sunlight. I walk along its periphery until, hours later, I arrive at a small resort that has a restaurant, closed for the season, and other buildings where swimmers can shower and change clothes. There are also several vendor stands, but only one is open and I see that it sells jewelry. I walk to it and happily greet a man who is sitting inside. I wonder if he's lonely, sitting on this stretch of beach by himself. When I ask him if he speaks English, he shakes his head. I point to a beaded necklace with jade-colored stones. He carefully picks it up and lays it in my hand.

"It's beautiful!" I tell him and pull out my pocketbook to buy it. I hand him 200 pesos, clasp the necklace around my neck, say, "*Muchas gracias*," and walk away. When I realize he's almost out of sight, I turn to him and wave.

I return to the hotel in the late afternoon and Mecha greets me at the door.

"Nico has been trying to reach you," she says. "He seems to be worried about you." I thank her, tell her I'm going to my room to rest and ask her where I should go for dinner.

"I'll tell you," she responds, placing her hand on my shoulder. "But first you should call Nico. Tell him you're OK."

I ask for his number and return to my room. I want to talk to him before I leave, but decide that it's best if I don't. After months of anticipation, days of lovemaking and miles of hiking, I feel emotionally and physically drained. I want to cry but I'm too tired. Instead, I lie on my bed, pull the covers over my head and quickly fall asleep.

It's nearly dark when I hear a tap at my door. I get up and open it. Nico is leaning against the doorframe.

"Kate, I'm glad you're OK; I was hoping you were here." I smile and invite him in, but instead he says, "Let's go for a drive, OK?" I nod.

"Let me brush my hair, I'll meet you downstairs," I say before closing the door. My heart is pounding since I'm so happy to see him but I'm resolute in my decision to return home. When I get outside, he's leaning on the hood of his truck and I pause for a moment. I want to remember his beauty after I am gone.

He opens the passenger door for me, and as I climb in, he says, "I promised I would show you the ski resort." I smooth my hair and fasten my seatbelt, trying hard not to cry. As he climbs into the truck, I tell him I hiked at Lácar Lake.

"Seriously?" he asks. "How did you figure out where to go?"

"It's not rocket science, Nico, you just follow the trail." When he raises his eyebrows as if to question me, I apologize. "Sorry, it's been a long day, I'm happy that you are taking me to the ski resort. Thank you."

We drive in silence and I try not to look at him. As we head into the mountains, I close my eyes and remember how he feels – so warm and so strong – and yearn to hold him close. I think about our time on the Chimehuin, how much I wanted him then and how much I want him now, so I fold my hands and place them in my lap. I don't want to reach for him.

When we pull into the ski resort, it's closed.

"It doesn't open until July," Nico explains, as he parks the truck. "But I want to show you something."

When we leave the truck, he takes my hand and my body tingles. We walk together for several yards before stopping at the top of a hill. The view is breathtaking; the Andes Mountains, now topped with snow, surround us, and in the distance is Lanín, just as I remember it, with clouds circling its crest and its very tip pointing to the darkening sky.

Nico and I stand together for several minutes before he speaks.

"I canceled the *asado*," he says, squeezing my hand. Because I can't believe what I've heard, I ask him to say it again.

"I canceled the *asado*, Kate. I don't want you to leave."

I turn to him and smile, placing my arms around his waist. I am so happy, so surprised, that I don't know what to say. Once again, I search for something neutral, something safe.

"I went to a milonga in Buenos Aires," I say. "Do you know what that is?"

"Yes," he replies, grinning. "It's a pick-up bar, but instead of talking first, you dance."

"That's true! Want to try it?" I try to sound encouraging. Still grinning, he takes a step back.

"I can't dance," he declares. "Actually, let me make myself more clear. I suck at dancing." I step closer.

"It's easy," I say, taking his hand in mine, "I learned before I got here. Let me show you." I place my other hand on his shoulder and stand facing him. His eyes sparkle and I wonder, "Is he crying?" I move close, feel him relax and look at our feet.

"We can do this," I coax, "even if it's not perfect."

"OK," he says, smiling, "but remember, I'm not that kind of guy."

I throw my head back and laugh. For the first time in days I feel free.

"We'll see!" I tell him as I begin to move. I point to the ground. "Set your left foot here and your right foot there."

He squeezes my hand and kisses my cheek.

"I love you, Kate," he says. "Let's just take this one step at a time."

I look at him, smile and pull him closer. I know he's not talking about dancing.

"I love you, too, Nico. I agree. Let's take this one step at a time. You start."

As Nico begins to move I follow, and soon he's humming a song. I fall easily into his rhythm, press my body against his and don't care what tomorrow will bring.

When he asks, "How'm I doing?" I say, "You're perfect!" and with Lanín towering behind us, we tango.

THE NEXT DAY I call Gus to tell him I won't be coming home. "I figured as much," he says. "Nico is a lucky guy."

Then, without skipping a beat, he reminds me that I owe him a feature story I've been writing about an American woman who left her "humdrum" life in the Chicago suburbs to move to Shanghai with her Chinese lover. "I get it," I remember telling the woman before my first trip to Patagonia. I promise Gus that I will send it soon.

And then he says he wants me to write about Argentina.

"Seriously?" I ask. "Why?" There's a pause on the line before he answers. I imagine that he's preparing to enlighten me, and he doesn't disappoint.

"Are you kidding me? Argentina? Political and economic instability? Inflation at nearly 40%? The new pope? Female president? The biggest dinosaur ever? That country is full of news.

You'll need something to do." Because I don't answer right away, he continues. "Kate, I know that you love Nico, but life there will not be easy for you. I want you to write about it because you will understand before you get in too deep."

I laugh before thanking him.

"What will I do without you?" I ask, tears welling up in my eyes.

"I don't know," he answers, "but I want the first story in one month. I'll pay you in advance when payroll deposits your check into your account. Watch for it." Without saying goodbye, he hangs up.

When I call Eva, she simply wants to know where I will live.

"Not sure," I tell her. "I'll ask Mecha to help me." After I hang up I call Andrew. He is surprisingly calm.

"It's the last time I teach a woman how to fish," he says with a curt laugh. I wait a few moments for him to speak again, and he does.

"Kate, I'm sorry if I was mean to you." I am so surprised by this that I nearly drop the phone. He continues, "If you ever decide you want to come back to Chicago, I'll lend you my jacket. Maybe we can watch the Thanksgiving parade together again."

I pause before answering, my heart aching for him.

"Andrew, thank you, I appreciate that. You know how I feel about Nico. I want to give this a chance. Please understand." Then we say our goodbyes.

Mecha finds me a small house on the outskirts of town near

the Chimehuin River with a septic system and Internet service. I realize I am taking a chance by staying, that Marina and her family might hate me and that they could make life difficult for Nico. He and I discuss this as we sit on a hillside early one morning to watch the sun rise over Lácar Lake.

"Patagonia is your home now, too," he says, wrapping his arm around my shoulders. "I want you to be happy here."

I kiss him gently on the mouth before turning to look at the twinkling lights of San Martín.

"I guess we'll just have to wait and see, Nico," I say, leaning my head on his shoulder. "We'll just have to wait and see." He stands up, takes my hand and pulls me close.

"You're safe with me," he says, smoothing my hair, "please don't worry." As I bury my face in his shoulder, I feel happy and choose not to think of what is to come.

PART II

CHAPTER 10

IMMERSE

It's dawn in Patagonia and I'm watching the deer graze on my neighbor Diego's lawn. Diego is also my Spanish tutor and we've become good friends. It hasn't rained for weeks and the ground is dry, but Diego, a fastidious slender man with dark curly hair and a bright smile, waters his lawn every day using spray bottles filled from a nearby well. As a result, his grass is green and tender, and each day before sunrise, a family of red deer arrives to eat it. Diego hates this, so every morning, wearing only boxer shorts, he runs from his house to chase the deer away, screaming, "*¡Fuera de aquí, canalla!* (Get out of here, scum)." As they run off, he turns and waves to me before heading back inside. He explained one day that rain in this part of Patagonia is "*oro líquido* (liquid gold)" and thus the deer are "*¡ladrones!* (thieves)."

"You know that Diego *likes* to feed the deer," says Nico as he walks from the bathroom, drying his wet curly hair with a thick white towel.

I turn to him and smile. He's leaving in an hour to guide and won't return for two weeks, but I decide there's time for us to make love again. I lie on the bed and pull him down next to me.

"Do you miss me when you're gone?" I ask, kissing him on his neck. He laughs and I roll on top of him as he wraps his arms around me. I reach down and place him inside of me. Minutes later, after we both climax, he responds.

"I have to leave, Kate. And yes, I do miss you."

I've been living in Patagonia for eight months and I've yet to see Marina or her family. When I first moved here in May, Nico and I trekked into the mountains, camped for days and made love beneath the stars. We rode mountain bikes near the ski resort and fished for trout in rivers and lakes. When winter came and the snow was heavy and relentless, I lived in Nico's house while he taught skiing through August. From the Internet I learned how to cook his favorite soups and stews. Because I didn't want to go to town, I had our groceries delivered. I was afraid to meet Nico's family for fear they wouldn't like me.

"Marina is unhappy with me," Nico told me one day as I was cooking *carbonada criolla*, an Argentine stew made with beef, sweet potatoes and winter squash. "She's not unhappy with you." Stirring the pot, I shook my head.

"I can't believe that. What woman would ever want to lose you, Nico? I just need time." He walked over and looked in the pot.

"Smells good," he said, "my mom makes this." After kissing me, he headed to the back door where Anabel was waiting to go outside.

"My parents will love you," he added before following Anabel out the door. "When are you going to meet them?" I answered him while slicing a baguette.

"After fishing season," I said, "in May."

In November when Nico began guiding, we lived at my house with Anabel. I spent most of my time walking with her, working at my computer or visiting with Diego, who decided when I first met him that I needed to learn Spanish.

"It's the language of romance," he explained while I watched him water his lawn. "Any woman from the U.S. who has an Argentine lover needs to know Spanish." I laughed.

"*Gracias mi amigo*," I said. "No kidding."

"Seriously," he added, "you need to be immersed." I tried not to smile.

"You mean in water?" I asked. He glared at me.

"No," he replied, "immersed in our culture, until you're finally Argentine."

He tutored me every day for weeks until we conversed only in Spanish, but instead of feeling accomplished, I felt homesick.

After Nico leaves, I walk into the bathroom. Thousands of tiny flies lie dead on the floor and I tiptoe around them.

"No-see-ums," I say to myself. "Yuck." I had forgotten to turn off the bathroom light before going to bed and Nico was already asleep. We long ago agreed to turn off the light at night when we opened the bathroom window so that the tiny flies, attracted to the light, wouldn't slip through the tiny holes in the screens.

"My bad," I say as I grab a roll of paper towels from under the sink. Wiping up the flies, I add under my breath, "No-see-ums – now I see you, now I don't" and toss them into the trash.

After showering I decide to take Anabel for a walk. I pull on a pair of shorts, a white tank top and ankle-high hiking boots and grab my cap from the kitchen counter. I slip two granola bars into a pocket and call Anabel, who has been sleeping near the back door. We head from the house in time to see Diego watering his lawn.

"*¿Sales a caminar?* (Going for a walk)," he shouts. I struggle to translate. "*¡Sí!*" I reply. "*¡Yo voy a dar un paseo!* (I am going for a walk)." He sets down his water bottle and thrusts his thumbs into the air. I do the same and smile. A thumbs-up means the same in all languages.

On the first day of our tutoring sessions, Diego met me at his front door, escorted me to the kitchen and gestured that I should sit at the kitchen table. A book titled, "*¿Sabías que....?*" was lying open on the table, along with a single tablet of paper and a pen.

"This is the last time that I speak in English to you," he said, pulling his chair close to the table. "You will learn more quickly if we just speak Spanish, OK? It's best that you learn how to converse with others. Do you understand?"

Eager to learn, I nodded. Over the next few days he used the book to teach me basic *vocabulario* and *gramática* and we quickly moved into full sentences. It was exhausting trying to translate past, present and future verbs into what "I, she, he, we, or they" did. Sometimes I would break into laughter while struggling to understand him and other days I would stomp around the room, angry at my stupidity.

One day he asked, "*¿En un restaurante, se te cae un tenedor. Que haces?* (In a restaurant, you drop a fork. What do you do)." I stared at him, trying hard to understand. I only recognized the word "restaurante."

"*¡Me muero de hambre!* (I'm starving)," I replied, and waited for his approval. Instead, he briskly shook his head, indicating that I was wrong. My throat tightened and I wanted to cry.

"*Monte mi bicicleta en el parque* (I ride my bike in the park)," I said, which we had agreed would be my "Plan B" phrase to indicate my frustration.

Diego, who had been pacing around the kitchen, stopped, looked at me and crossed his arms.

"Kate," he said, "did you think this would be easy?" I grinned at his English and wiped my eyes.

"Yes," I replied, "actually, I did."

Patagonia's climate is dry and today I feel it. Having walked miles and miles, my throat is parched and I've already drained my water bottle. I look at Anabel, who is running around me and panting, and point her down a dirt road that leads to the Chimehuin.

"Going to fill my water bottle," I explain, reaching to rub her head, "and you can drink, too."

"Giardia," Eva warned me in an email when I wrote to her about these walks and the fact that I filled my bottle from the river.

"Wait, let me be more specific," she wrote, "violent diarrhea."

Today I ignore her, figuring it's better than dehydration.

When I reach the bank, Anabel takes off to chase a nearby cow and I scan the area. It's beautiful here, peaceful and calm except for the occasional rising fish and squawking bird. A snowy egret, its white plumage bright against the dark green willows, is standing still on the bank, hunting for fish. It looks like a statue. Diego taught me that the Spanish name for a snowy egret is *garcita blanca* and I whisper that while watching. Then Anabel, her coat covered with large burrs, runs up to me and barks and the egret flies away.

"There you go, sweet girl," I tell her, "now you see it, now you don't."

Because I am alone with hours of silence, I have more time to think about my childhood. While taking a nap, I had a nightmare in which my mother, who was drunk, beat me for not telling her that I would be home late from school. This actually happened. I was 14 and had tiptoed into the house while she lay passed out on the couch, thinking I was safe. When she awoke and lunged at me, I closed my eyes and tried to block out the pain and humiliation. These beatings happened often, always when my sister and brother were away at school or playing with friends. I was too ashamed to tell anyone and buried my feelings deeper and deeper, suffering in silence until I started dating Clay. Recognizing that my mother was an alcoholic, he encouraged me to stay at his house where his mother fed me dinner and bought me new clothes. When my mother would call to tell me to come home, Clay told her to leave me alone. After Clay and I married, I never saw her again.

The first time Nico left for guiding, he encouraged me to visit a nearby estancia named Hermosas Montañas to meet his friends Fede and Nidra.

"Hermosas Montañas means beautiful mountains," he explained. "Nidra will feed you and Fede will take you riding in the mountains, just like we did when we saw the condors."

Today after I leave the river, I decide to take his advice and stop at the gate that leads to the lodge. Constructed of giant logs, it has a large sign that says Hermosas Montañas hanging from its top.

Anabel and I gingerly walk through the gate across a homemade cattle grate onto a dirt road that winds alongside a pasture where horses are grazing. Anabel charges up to them and barks, but because they ignore her, she returns to follow me. Several minutes later, I see the lodge, which is nearly camouflaged by a large grove of poplars. Next to the lodge is a stable, where a man wearing gaucho clothes and a beret is grooming a large brown horse. The horse is munching on hay from a loosened bale on the ground.

"*¡Buenas tardes!*" I yell. The man turns to me, smiles and walks over.

"*¡Hola señorita!*" he yells back as the horse snorts and whinnies. "*¿Puedo ayudarte?* (Can I help you)."

Anabel runs to the horse and barks. Like the horses in the pasture, it ignores her, so she heads to a flock of sheep that are drinking from a nearby pond. When they see her, they scatter.

Nodding toward Anabel, I look at the man and smile.

"*Sí, señor, ¿cómo estás? ¿Habla usted Inglés?*" The man removes his cap and bows.

"Ah, you must be Kate. Welcome to Patagonia. We were wondering when we would see you."

I hear a door slam in the distance and turn around. A slender woman with long dark hair is striding toward us from the lodge, waving.

"*¡Hola!*" she calls out. "Fede, is this Kate?" The man nods.

"That's Nidra," he explains. "She has wanted to meet you for months."

Before I left Chicago, Eva gave me a delicate silver necklace with a tiny cross. At its center was a single garnet, my birthstone. "You'll need this," she said, "if for no other reason than to fit in with the Catholics."

I smiled at her as I clasped the necklace around my neck and ran my fingers over the cross. "I love it!" I said. "And I'll never take if off. It will remind me of you."

She gave me a hug before looking at me, her hands on my shoulders. "If it doesn't work out there, you can always come home and live with me and Jason. You know that, right?"

I hugged her back. "I'm not coming home," I told her, "because I know it will work out."

Nidra sees my necklace when she hugs me.

"Welcome!" she cries. "It's so good to finally meet you! What a beautiful necklace! Please, come inside and have coffee and cakes." I turn to Fede as I walk.

"*¡Hasta luego!*" I call out, but he's already back at his post, grooming the horse.

We walk to the lodge, which is painted apple green and has white shutters on both sides of each window. A sidewalk winds alongside it and is bordered by red rose bushes and various ornamental grasses.

"This is beautiful," I tell Nidra as she escorts me inside.

"Yes, we like it here," she responds. "Please make yourself comfortable. I'll get the coffee. Do you take cream and sugar?"

"No," I answer, "just black, thank you."

As she walks away I watch her, wondering if she's Argentine or Indian. I ask her as she returns with the coffee and cakes, which are set on an ornate brass tray. She sets the tray on a table before answering.

"I was born in Mumbai," she says, pouring coffee into my cup. "I met Fede in Buenos Aires when we were both in college there. He wanted me to move here with him and I told him, 'Not on your life,' but here I am, 20 years later, happy as a clam."

I pick up my cup and sip the coffee. It tastes rich and hot.

"What's your secret?" I ask as she watches me.

She pauses for several seconds before answering and picks up a cake with pink icing.

"No secret," she answers, taking a bite of the cake. "It's beautiful here and so are the people; you'll see." We drink and eat for a moment before she speaks again. "Is Nico guiding?"

I set down my cup, pick up a napkin and wipe my hands.

"Yes. He won't be home for two weeks." She smiles at me before continuing.

"He and Fede are good friends. He told Fede he was so happy when he met you."

I'm surprised. I never thought Nico would tell his friends about me, instead figuring that he would keep our relationship secret to protect Marina.

"Thank you," I say, leaning back on the couch. "I was happy when I met him, too."

Nidra and I talk for over an hour about Chicago and Mumbai. I ask about her family.

"They came here last year," she says, "but they say it's boring." I smile at her and nod my head.

"I agree," I say. "At first I was bored, now I walk. Sometimes I fish."

Nidra looks at me with her eyes wide.

"Fish?" she asks. "Did Nico teach you?"

I look away and pick up my cup. It's empty, so I set it down.

"No, an old friend taught me, in Chicago, a long time ago." I swallow hard.

Nidra smiles and shakes her head.

"I never learned to fly-fish; maybe someday you could teach me."

Wiping my eyes with my napkin, I change the subject.

"Nidra is a beautiful name, what does it mean?"

"Ha!" she says, "It means 'Goddess of Sleep,' but unfortunately, I don't get any sleep around here; there's always something to do." I think of Eva and how she would love knowing the Goddess of Sleep.

"We have guests here from all over the world," she continues. "They even come from Europe and Asia. I enjoy meeting different cultures, but my favorite culture is in Argentina. The people here are incredibly friendly and accepting." The front door opens and we turn our heads and see Fede, who's removing his beret.

"Ladies," he announces, bowing again, "sorry to interrupt, but Nico is outside."

CHAPTER 11
CELEBRATE

I jump up from the couch, look out the window and see Nico as he climbs from his truck. I run from the house, down the driveway and jump into his arms, wrapping my legs around his waist and pulling off his cap so that I can feel his hair. I'm so happy that I can barely breathe.

"Oh my God," I exclaim, "you're here!"

Laughing, he kisses me and I taste dust on his lips. Because his clothes are stained, I know he's just left the river. I'm surprised to see him so soon.

"Client got sick," he says, leaning back to look at me, "so I decided to come home."

We stare at each other for a moment before he speaks again.

"And," he adds, "I missed you." I smile and hug him as I hear Nidra and Fede walk up behind us.

"Nicolás!" shouts Fede. "*¿Cómo estás amigo?* (How are you, my friend)."

Nico kneels to pet Anabel, who has left the sheep to greet him.

"Good!" he answers. "I see that you've met Kate." Nidra walks over and puts her arm over my shoulders.

"Yes," she says, "we're good friends now. Want to stay for dinner?" Nico stands to look at us before speaking.

"No," he replies, "I'm taking Kate out to eat. It's her birthday tomorrow."

Surprised that he remembers, I walk over and hug him. The only other person who celebrates my birthday is Eva.

"I love you," I whisper in his ear. He kisses me on the cheek.

"Another time?" he asks Fede.

Fede puts his arm around Nidra's shoulder and kisses her on the cheek.

"Yes, of course, have fun and please take your dog with you. She's about to eat the sheep."

As Nico and I get into the truck, he turns to me.

"I hope it's OK that we don't stay with them. I want you to see something." I'm reminded of the time he first drove me into the mountains to show me the twinkling lights of San Martín.

"Yes," I tell him, taking his hand, "I want to be alone with you."

We drive for several miles until we reach the mountains. The evening is calm with only a slight breeze and the sun is setting, bathing the landscape in golden light. Anabel is asleep in the back seat and Nico and I ride in silence, holding hands. I think about our first time together on the Chimehuin and how we slept in each other's arms until dusk, so I squeeze his hand. I'm just beginning to know him. He's such a strong man and so handsome, funny and smart. I know that he gets tired from trying to please his clients and from rowing the boat and retrieving the fish. Tonight, as on most nights, I'll massage his back, shoulders and neck until he falls asleep, and then tuck myself in beside him, feeling safe, secure and loved. I'm so glad that he's home.

By the time we reach our destination it's nearly dark. Nico climbs from the truck, walks quickly to my door, opens it, and leads me to a clearing where there's a blanket on the ground surrounded by at least a dozen unlit candles. A large cooler sits on the ground nearby.

"Happy birthday, Kate," he says, wrapping his arm around my waist. "Happy birthday."

I look at him, stunned. When did he have time to do this? He takes a book of matches from his pocket and begins to light the candles while I watch. Then he opens the cooler and removes several containers of food, two bottles of wine and two crystal wine glasses, each wrapped in a paper towel.

"I didn't want them to break," he explains while unwrapping them. I lean over to help.

"It's all so beautiful," I whisper. "I don't know what else to say."

"Then say nothing," he responds, leading me to a pillow. "Sit down and I'll pour us some wine. We're about to make a toast."

Andrew never liked to toast. "It's for people with nothing important to say," he told me one night at dinner when I held up my glass. "But if you really want to, I'll do it." I set down my glass and shook my head.

"No problem," I said, picking up my fork. "Let's just eat."

Andrew had made lasagna and we ate in silence. It was only days after our first fishing trip and we were making plans to move in together.

"Are you sure you want to do this?" he asked. I wasn't sure, but felt pulled to do it. I wasn't used to being assertive unless I was interviewing – it was easy to hide behind my reporter's notebook. Andrew, on the other hand, was assertive, and I liked this about him since it was a piece of my puzzle that was missing. I lost it when my father died.

"To us," says Nico, extending his wine glass. We touch the glasses together and I drink while he removes the lids from the containers of food. As my eyes adjust to the dark I see fried chicken, potato salad, sausages, cheese, and olives. Anabel is lying beside me, sleeping. I lightly stroke her head.

"And to Anabel," he adds. I smile.

I scoop potato salad onto his plate and hand him a piece of fried chicken. As we eat, candles flickering around us, he asks me about my day.

"I'm glad you met Fede and Nidra," he says, pouring more wine into my glass. "You like them, yes?" I nod as I drink and he hands me a piece of chicken. I take a bite.

"Yes," I reply, chewing, "a lot."

Nico wipes his hands with a napkin, lies facing me on the ground and folds his arms beneath his head. I love this about him; he can relax anywhere on Patagonia's rough terrain, and while guiding often siestas on the ground beneath the trees after lunch, his fishing cap covering his face.

"Have you given any more thought to meeting my parents?" he asks, clearing his throat. I sip my wine and look at him.

"I guess after nearly a year it makes sense, doesn't it?" I reply, wrinkling my nose.

Nico jumps up, grabs my hand and pulls me close. Startled, Anabel looks up, yawns and, reassured that we're all right, falls back asleep.

"I was hoping you would say that," he sings, guiding us in an awkward tango. "I know that they'll love you as much as I do."

We eat and drink until midnight. Nico packs the remaining food into his truck before pulling two sleeping bags from the back seat. We blow out the candles, zip the bags together and snuggle, naked, inside. The night is quiet and we stare at the moon, imagining what's there.

"Mountains and lakes and thousands of fish," says Nico, yawning.

"No," I declare, putting my head on his shoulder as he begins to snore. "Castles and princesses and giant dragons that protect them from the bad guys. That," I whisper before falling asleep, "is what lives there."

Early the next morning we drive home. When we arrive, we see an unfamiliar truck parked in the driveway.

"Odd," I say as we walk toward it. "Do you know who it is?" Nico waves his hands, indicating that I should walk behind him.

"Not sure," he replies, "let me handle it."

Anabel starts to bark, runs around the truck and the driver's door opens. It's Mike.

"There you are!" he cries as he walks toward us. I haven't seen Mike in months so run and hug him. Since he's wearing fishing clothes and waders, I know what's coming next.

"We need you back on the river, buddy," he says to Nico, who's grinning. "Sorry to interrupt your morning."

I feel sorry for Nico, but even sorrier for me.

"OK," he tells Mike as he unpacks our truck. "Give me a minute while I take these things inside."

After Nico disappears into the house, Mike removes his fishing cap.

"Want to go with us?" he asks, rubbing his head. "It's your birthday gift. Collon Cura River this time. It's supposed to be a surprise, but I'm not good at keeping secrets."

I open my mouth in mock disapproval, and then I laugh.

"Seriously? Yes! Give me a sec!" I run down the driveway to the house and see Diego watering his lawn. He's watching me, so I shout, "I mean, ¡sí, sí, sí, dame un segundo! (Give me a second)." He drops his water bottle and gives me a thumbs-up. I wave.

January in Patagonia is warm and windy, and on the rivers, the inchworms rule. Tiny and green, they live in willow trees and stick to the leaves, devouring them before dropping onto the water. When the trout see the inchworms, they eat them, so today after we arrive at the Collon Cura, Nico ties an inchworm fly onto my tippet.

"You'll have fun with this, Kate," he mumbles as he tightens the knot with his teeth. "You'll see."

Mike is pulling the boat from the trailer and pushes it into the water.

"Inchworms, you hungry fish!" he yells. "Come an' get 'em!"

I pull on my wading boots, climb into the boat and sit in front. Nico sits in back. I'm excited to fish with him again, remembering his perfect cast and how generous he was to teach Eva how to fish. My love for him gets stronger every day, so I turn in my seat to look at him and am surprised to see him looking at me.

We stare at each other for a moment, smiling.

"*Eres hermosa, mi amor* (You are beautiful, my love)," he says and blows me a kiss. I catch the invisible kiss in my hand and tuck it into my pocket.

"*Gracias, mi amor. Eres hermoso, también* (Thank you, my love. You are beautiful, too)." Mike starts rowing.

"You guys are so cute," he says. "Now let's see you catch some fish."

Legends abound in Patagonia about the largest trout caught, and today we look for a giant brown.

"They hide beneath the willows and catch the inchworms as

soon as they fall," explains Mike, nodding toward the shoreline. "That's how they get so big."

I tell him I think this is funny, that the trout would be so smart.

"OK," says Nico to Mike, "let's show her."

Nico tells Mike to row to the bank. There's a calm pool nearby being fed by the river through a deep and powerful eddy. The rushing water is so loud I can barely hear Nico when he calls to me.

"Kate!" he shouts, tucking his net into his belt. "Your big brown lives over there!" He's pointing to a giant willow growing in the corner of the pool next to a rock outcropping that blocks the shoreline. The willow is surrounded by tall underbrush and casts a giant shadow on the water, which is covered with bright green inchworms. I smile. Trout that live there are well fed *and* protected. Smart.

I climb from the boat to get a closer look and Nico follows. He hands me my rod.

"There's an enormous brown trout right there," he shouts, pointing to the shadowy water. "I want you to cast beyond it and slowly work your way under the branches where it's eating."

I squint to find the fish, but the water is so dark that I can't see anything. Trusting Nico, I step into the eddy as Mike watches from the boat. The water is flowing so fast that I can barely stand, so I grind my boots into the gravel and Nico grabs my arm. I look at the willow and strategize; to land the fish, I need to lead it from the tree to the quiet pool. Steadying myself, I pull several feet of line from my reel and cast to the tree, but it's so windy that the line whips behind me. I have trouble pulling it forward.

"Remember, power in your back cast!" shouts Nico, though I can barely hear him above the wind. "Just take your time!" He grips the back of my jacket to help me stand and I cast again. This time I snag a low-lying branch but pull the line free without losing the fly.

On my third cast, the fly finally hits the water and within moments, a fish pulls it down. I'm so surprised by this that at first, I do nothing.

"Set!" shouts Nico. "Set!" I jerk the rod up and feel the fish. It's heavy and takes off, first closer to the tree, then across the eddy.

"Let it run!" he shouts, still holding my jacket. "Let it run! And wade! I've got you!"

The fish pulls so hard that I need to hold the rod with both hands. I strip the line through my fingers and they burn. Determined, I wade to the gravel bar next to the pool and pull the fish toward me. When it finally fords the eddy and darts into calmer water, I see it, but only briefly before it dives deep. It's a big brown trout.

I'm so excited that I want to scream but I laugh instead.

"This is so much fun!" I shriek. "So much fun!" A few minutes later the fish rolls onto its side and I pull it to the gravel bar, careful to leave it in the water.

"Big fish!" shouts Nico, grabbing the net from his belt. He scoops the fish into the net and moments later, gently removes it. Holding it by the tail, he measures it against the handle, which is marked like a ruler. The fish is calm.

"Twenty-six inches!" he calls to Mike. "Biggest fish of the season!" He gently returns the fish to the water, slowly gliding it back and forth to ensure that water is flowing through its gills. A few seconds after it's revived, it swims away.

Nico stands and tucks the net into his belt. He looks at me and grins.

"Now do you believe that there are giant fish in the river?" he asks.

"Yes!" I squeal, jumping into his arms. "Enormous! Enormous!" I kiss him and wrap my legs around his waist. He carries me back to the boat and Mike, who has been watching us, laughs.

"Hey, Kate," he says, "what was more challenging? Catching Nico or catching that fish?" As Nico sets me down in the boat, I wrinkle my nose at him and smile. I decide to say nothing.

We get home at dusk and wave to Mike as he drives away. None of us caught fish after my big brown, but it didn't matter. We ended the day happy and exhausted. When Nico opens the front door, Anabel runs out, barking. We peel off our clothes, fall into bed and listen to Anabel as she howls at the moon.

"*Feliz cumpleaños* (Happy birthday), Kate," says Nico, turning to me. "*Te amo* (I love you)."

I reach out to him and he pulls me close. As Anabel howls, we fall asleep.

The next morning, I wake early to work on an article for Gus, but my computer is dead. I check email on my phone.

"Where's that article about the pope?" Gus writes. His email is from yesterday. "And BTW, are you surviving your little adventure in Argentina?"

I choose not to answer him, so I lay my phone on the kitchen table. A few seconds later, it's pinging with WhatsApp text messages and I check the screen. It's Gus.

"F*** Kate! Why arnt you reading yur emails! We need to tlk! Argtina is all over the nws!"

I smile. He hasn't changed one bit. How does he survive without me? I text him back.

"Got it, sorry, computer battery is dead. I'll call you tonight from town. We don't have a good signal here."

After I send it, I realize what I've done. I don't want to go to town. What if I see Marina?

I return to the bedroom to lie next to Nico, who's just waking up. He rolls onto his stomach and lays his arm on my chest. I rub his shoulder and gently touch his beard and he opens one eye.

"Gus?" he asks, staring at me.

"How did you guess?" I answer. I take his hand in mine and turn it over so that I can see his palm. It's dotted with calluses, so I lean over to my night table, pull out a small container of oil and dab a bit in my palm. As I rub it over his calluses, he smiles and yawns.

"How am I so lucky?" he asks, sleepily.

"You're not lucky," I tell him, "this is because you're so amazing."

We don't mention Gus again until we're in the kitchen preparing breakfast. Nico has the day off, and we're scheduled to ride horses at Hermosas Montañas. While he slices bacon, I prepare eggs for scrambling. The sun is shining; a perfect day, and as Nico lays the bacon into the frying pan, I tell him that I need to go to town.

"Nico, you know that story I wrote about the pope?" He nods.

"Yes, what about it? Is that why Gus texted you?"

I set aside the eggs and begin to slice oranges, placing each segment onto a platter. Coffee is steeping in our French press and Anabel is sleeping on the back porch.

"Yes," I respond, "I need to go to town to talk to him."

Nico tosses the empty bacon package into the trash and stares at me.

"Seriously?" he asks. "Today? That's great. What time? Now?"

I can tell that he wants me to meet his parents.

"No, not now," I tell him, "Gus can wait. Let's eat breakfast and ride those horses."

When I first met Gus, I felt intimidated. My father was a quiet man and controlled by my mother and rarely disagreed with anything she said. Gus, on the other hand, was not shy about speaking his mind. As a young girl, I had dreamed of living in Chicago, thinking one day I would marry a rich man, wear high heels and carry a Chanel purse while strolling down Michigan Avenue. That didn't happen. Instead, on the day I interviewed with Gus, I sat in a grimy newsroom with yellowed newspapers stacked on every surface. I watched as editors shouted at the reporters and the reporters shouted back. All of them were drinking coffee out of Styrofoam cups.

"Why do you want to be a journalist?" asked Gus when he finally got around to talking to me. We were sitting at his gunmetal gray desk, which was twice the size of a normal desk and rusting at the seams. He called it his battleship.

"I don't know," I responded. "I guess I want to make a difference."

He smiled. "You know, that's what everyone says. You'll need to be more creative when you're working for me. When can you start?"

When Nico and I arrive at Hermosas Montañas, our horses are ready to ride. I tell Nidra about Gus.

"It must be torture for him not to hear from you," she laughs as she helps me into the saddle. "What did you say about the pope?"

"Nothing really," I tell her. "It's a puff piece. The article I'm working on now is about the cinder block shanties. How can people stand to live like that?"

Nidra frowns at me as she adjusts my stirrups.

"Those people are quite poor," she admonishes. "For some people, the cinder block homes are like the Taj Mahal. I hope you wrote about that in your article."

I had. When my computer was working, I scoured the Internet reading about the president's welfare system. I also read about Argentina's history. I was captivated by its opulence before hardship, and distressed to read about the Dirty War when, under President Jorge Rafael Videla, a three-man military junta closed the National Congress, imposed censorship, banned trade unions, and brought state and municipal government under military control. Dissidents were sent to detention camps, and ultimately between 10,000 and 30,000 citizens were seized by authorities and never heard from again. It was rumored that they were killed. With this backdrop, I marveled at the resilience of people like Nico who worked hard yet were victim to the country's rampant inflation.

As Nico and I ride around the estancia, we discuss this in Spanish. I start.

"Nico, *cuánto tiempo tienen que sufrir las buenas personas* (How long do good people have to suffer)?"

"Ah!" he replies. "*¡En español! Hasta que la gente buena este a cargo* (Until the good people are in charge)." He waits for me to translate.

"Ah, *sí*," I say, "*esas buenas personas sos vos* Nico (Those good people would be you, Nico).” When he indicates that I should continue, I speak again, this time in English.

“Seriously, Nico, you could make good things happen. You're strong and smart. Argentina needs someone like you to be in charge.”

He's quiet as he guides his horse near mine.

“Thank you,” he says, patting the horse's neck, “but it's a huge job, Kate. I do what I can here by keeping my family strong and by entertaining clients who want to experience this place.” I start to speak but he stops me. “And I do what I can to make you happy, Kate. Are you happy?” I lean over and touch his leg.

“Yes,” I reply, with my hand on his thigh. “I don't think I've ever been happier in my life.”

THAT NIGHT, Nico drives me to town and teases that we're visiting “under the cloak of darkness, like Batman.” I know he's right. I figure that no one will see me and that once we find a strong telephone signal, I can just call Gus without leaving my seat.

But soon it seems like everyone in town knows Nico's truck. As we drive, cars beep and headlights flash and Nico waves at them all. On Avenue San Martín, people walking on the sidewalks wave at him and call his name. Then his phone rings.

He speaks quickly to the caller in Spanish.

“My mom,” he mouths before hanging up. He tucks the phone in his pocket. “She wants me to bring you over.”

CHAPTER 12
EMERGE

Meeting Nico's mother was the last thing I wanted to do. What if I learned to love her and he dumped me? What if I wasn't good enough? What if my Spanish was terrible? And worse, what if she and I became so close that she would want to know about *my* mother? Riding in Nico's truck I feel my cheeks get warm. The shame of my childhood is suffocating me like a soiled garbage bag pulled tight around my neck.

"Now?" I ask him, smoothing my hair. "Now?"

He pulls the truck to the curb, shifts it into park and leans toward me.

"Kate," he says, "we can't keep pretending like this is a first date, right?" His beautiful, expressive green eyes are narrowed and I swallow hard to keep from crying. I feel a tear seep from my right eye and he wipes it away with his little finger.

"I love you, Kate. My family knows that. Why is this so difficult?"

I've never told Nico about my mom and her inability to cope after my father died. I've never told him that she beat me. Tonight I still hide it.

"I'm not Argentine, but I know that's not a good excuse. I'm sorry to be a pain."

He shifts the gear into drive and checks the side mirror before pulling onto the street.

"All right then," he says, "I'll call her to tell her we're on our way. Meanwhile, why don't you call Gus?"

Gus answers on the first ring.

"There you are!" he shouts into the phone. "What took you so long?" I pull the phone from my ear and speak into the microphone.

"You don't need to yell, Gus, I can hear you just fine. I'm only in South America, not on another planet."

When I hear Gus's swivel chair squeaking in the background, I know he's rolling across the floor to shut his office door.

"Better?" he asks more quietly.

"Yes," I answer. He pauses before continuing.

"How's life beneath the equator?"

I smile. Gus always puts me in a better mood.

"Hot and dry," I tell him. "What do you need? Nico and I are driving to meet his parents. I need to hang up soon."

I hear a snort and realize that Gus is laughing.

"Parents? Already? Sounds serious. How's it going?"

"It's going just fine," I say, impatiently. "Gus, you asked me to call you and I'm calling you. Did you like the story?"

I hear him typing on his computer and I figure he's pulling up my article.

"Perfect!" he says as he finishes typing. "Cinder blocks? Can you get a picture?"

I look at Nico and smile. To Gus I say, "I'll ask Lola to do it."

Gus takes a deep breath before shouting into the phone.

"Who the hell is Lola?" I pause since I know he'll apologize. "Sorry," he adds, "is that the woman who picks you up at the airport? Does she have a camera?"

I roll my eyes. Gus is a bit out of touch.

"Yes, Lola has a camera, two iPhones, four PCs, and a Mac laptop. She runs a tourist business in Buenos Aires, which is not like Mayberry. She knows what she's doing."

Gus laughs and I hear someone walk into his office.

"OK, I have to run," he shouts, "but I want you to look into something. Apparently there's this underground money exchange thing going on down there. You know, where the locals are taking advantage of the U.S. visitors. Exchanging our dollars for counterfeit pesos. I want you to investigate. Ask Nico. Maybe he knows something."

Nico is turning the truck onto a quiet street, so I tell Gus that I need to hang up.

"OK, I'll think about it. Right now I really need to leave."

We say goodbye just as Nico is parking his truck.

"We're here," he says, leaning over to kiss me. I push him away and open my purse.

"Wait!" I cry. "I need to brush my hair!"

"OK," he says, "but you already look great."

At that moment, I realize I love him even more. I reach over and hug him.

"Thank you for accepting me," I tell him. "I love you very much."

We hold hands as we walk to the front door, but before we can knock, it swings open. A petite woman with shoulder-length auburn hair takes our hands and pulls us inside. She's wearing a turquoise dress and bright orange scarf, and she hugs me. Her hair smells like jasmine.

"Kate! Nico has told me all about you. Welcome! I am very, very happy to meet you!"

When she stands back, I see that her eyes are the same color as Nico's. I presume that she's his mother.

"I am happy to meet you, too!" I respond. "I'm sorry that we didn't tell you earlier that we would be in town."

The woman waves her hand and scoffs.

"Nicolás, why don't you take Kate's jacket, and let's go into the living room. I have wine and snacks." I watch as she walks away.

"That's my mom," says Nico. "Julieta Luisa."

As we move into the living room, I look around, and Nico pours the wine. The walls are covered with framed photographs showing groups of happy people standing next to lakes, on bikes, in rafts, and at *asados*. There are dozens of formal portraits and school photographs as well; I decide that one is of Nico since the boy in the photo has voluminous green eyes. Family, I think to myself, feeling wistful.

When I hear Julieta speak from the living room, I walk toward her.

"Please, in here," she says, gesturing to a large stuffed sofa. "Make yourself at home."

I sit on the sofa just as Nico's father enters the room. He's tall and slender and his short hair is dark with streaks of gray. When he smiles at me, I realize that this is what Nico will look like when he gets older. He speaks to Julieta in Spanish and she turns to me.

"Kate," she says, "this is Nico's father, Franco. He does not speak English, but he wanted me to tell you that you are beautiful."

I never thought of myself as beautiful. "When will you stop wearing clothes like you're an old hippie?" asked Andrew one night when we were dressing to meet his law partners and wives for dinner in Greektown.

I was brushing my hair but stopped and turned to look at him.

"Sorry?" I asked. "Did you say something about my clothes?" I was dumbfounded. The only other person who spoke to me like that was my mother, and she was dead.

"Yes," said Andrew, buttoning his shirt. "You're a beautiful woman, Kate, why don't you invest in some nicer clothes? We can afford it." I didn't know what to say; I felt as if he were giving me a backhanded compliment. He added, "Seriously, you shouldn't be wearing that, the wives will be wearing dresses."

I felt my throat tighten and looked in the mirror at what I was wearing: designer jeans, a white blouse and long beaded necklace.

I now felt unfashionable and ugly.

"OK," I told him, running to the closet, "no problem, I'll change."

Julieta asks me if I like San Martín.

"Yes," I answer, munching on an empanada. It's still warm.

"One day Nico will need to take you to Gaiman near the east coast of Patagonia," she continues. "They have a Welsh bakery there with wonderful teas and cakes. It was Princess Diana's favorite place to visit when she came to Argentina."

After finishing the empanada I sip my wine and watch Nico. He and Franco are talking in Spanish and it must be something funny since both are laughing. I turn to Julieta. She's watching me.

"Did people in the U.S. like Princess Diana?" she asks. I stare at her for a moment before responding.

"Yes," I answer, picking up a slice of cheese and placing it on a cracker. "I think most people liked her. I especially liked her for standing up against the prince's affair with Camilla, you know?"

Julieta tilts her head as if trying to understand.

"But," I add, "it looks like the prince loved Camilla more than he loved Diana. You know, love always wins out in the end, I guess."

I begin to take a bite of the cracker and realize that the room is silent. Nico and his father are watching me, and after a moment, Julieta smiles.

"Yes," she says, "I guess love does always win in the end, even when there's a commitment to another."

I watch her and wonder if she's talking about Marina and me. Did I say something wrong?

I glance at Nico, who's standing up from the couch.

"I should take you to Gaiman?" he asks, stretching. I glance at his stomach, which is now exposed beneath his shirt; I love to rest my hand there after we make love.

"You'll like the food at the tea house," he continues. "Maybe they'll teach you how to bake those cakes!"

I smile at him, grateful that he's changing the subject, and Julieta laughs.

"Nico!" she exclaims. "*You* could learn how to bake those cakes!" She turns to me and asks, "Do you like to bake, Kate?" I nod my head.

"Do empanadas count as baking?" I ask, smiling. "Or is that cooking? I make them for us all the time."

I expect Julieta to laugh at me, but instead she puts her finger to her lips for a moment as if thinking.

"You know, Kate," she says, when she finally speaks, "that's a good point. I really don't know."

When Nico and I get home, he carries me to the bedroom and playfully tosses me on the bed.

"Camilla and Princess Diana? Tea and cakes?" He's laughing.

"I guess you didn't want to talk about fishing!"

He's undressing and grinning at me. I want to feel happy but mostly I feel relieved.

When he's naked, he lies next to me. Still grinning, he lifts my shirt and caresses my stomach with his index finger. My skin is immediately covered with goose bumps. I am aroused.

"I'm not sure how I feel about making love right after we've met your parents," I tell him, pulling my shirt over my head. "But since you insist, I can be persuaded."

The next day Nico leaves to guide for two weeks and I spend more time with Nidra. Hermosas Montañas is nearly 60,000 acres with 10,000 sheep, 300 cows and 70 horses, so there is much to do. While Fede manages the stable and livestock, Nidra manages the lodge and kitchen, does all the bookkeeping, handles all reservations, bartends, and entertains. Her incredible energy never seems to wane. She is also intelligent and well educated. When she met Fede, she was in graduate school at the University of Buenos Aires studying urban and regional planning, having received her undergraduate degree in civil engineering at the Indian Institute of Technology Bombay.

One day I ask her why she never pursued engineering as a career.

"I love meeting new people," she answers while fluffing the huge white pillows on the couches in the living room. "Most who come to Patagonia are adventurous and strong, like you."

I smile at her and say nothing, thinking about the article that

I just sent to Gus about Argentine President Cristina Fernández de Kirchner introducing a 50-peso bill designed with an image of the Malvinas Islands. The intent, said Cristina, was to honor the 649 Argentine soldiers who lost their lives during the South Atlantic conflict with the United Kingdom. I tell Nidra about the article after she's moved from fluffing the pillows to organizing the liquor bottles behind the bar.

"I wonder who does Cristina's makeup?" she asks absentmindedly while checking the bottles. "What do you think? Should I put these in alphabetical order? It might make things easier." I laugh at her ability to focus on the moment. She doesn't take anything too seriously, including politics.

I decide to ask her about the counterfeit pesos.

"Gus wants me to write about some sort of counterfeit peso ring in this part of Argentina. Do you know anything about it?"

She turns and looks at me but doesn't answer. A server opens the kitchen's swinging door and begins to dry wine glasses, carefully setting each glass into an ornate wooden cabinet near the bar. Otherwise, the room is quiet. I begin to feel uncomfortable in the silence and Nidra must sense it since she gestures for me to move closer. She speaks in a near whisper.

"Fede heard about those pesos during the *asado* that he goes to each week with Marina's brothers and uncles. Nico usually goes, too, but he hasn't been there for a while. Not since he met you."

I nod. So there is something going on. Why hasn't Nico told me? And why has he stopped going to the *asados*?

Nidra changes the subject.

"Just a few more weeks before we're closed, thank God!" she says, walking away.

I follow her and decide not to ask for more details about the pesos. Since Fede's involved, I don't want to use Nidra as a source.

She leads me to the kitchen where she pulls two Dansk mugs from a cabinet. They're white with blue rims. After setting them on the counter, she opens a window.

"I love the warm air," she says as she pours coffee into the mugs. "I am not looking forward to winter."

Nidra and Fede live in the mountains during the winter, where they both ski.

"Funny that an Indian girl would ski, yes?" she asks as she sips her coffee. "Being born and raised in Mumbai, I never feel warm in the winter, but that's how much I love Fede."

My thoughts about the counterfeit pesos are lingering in the back of my mind, but I push them away. Nidra clearly doesn't want to discuss it so I tell her that I met Nico's family.

She winks at me as she sips from her cup.

"Way to go! I know you were nervous about that. Do you like them? More importantly, do they like you?"

Nidra and I had long ago exhausted the topic of Nico and his family. I told her that I didn't want to know them in case my relationship with Nico didn't work out.

"Seriously?" she asked. "Clearly, he's crazy about you."

I told her about Clay and Andrew and that I never felt about them the way I feel about Nico.

"I love falling asleep with him every night and waking up with him every morning," I told her. "And I feel less guarded than ever before."

"Ah," she said. "To use a terrible analogy, it sounds like when you fell in love with Nico your feelings emerged like a fish from the water. Maybe the timing was just right."

The first day of winter arrives with a snowstorm. Nico and I are moving into his house since he'll teach skiing. When we arrive, we begin to unpack the stacks of boxes sitting in the bed of his truck. As I carry a box to the front door, a snowball hits my shoulder. Looking up, I see Nico standing in the yard, preparing another. His grin is devious.

"Ha!" I scream, setting the box on the porch and running to the backyard. "No way!"

Laughing, I find a snowbank and hide, but know that I'm only buying time since Nico will follow my tracks. Plus, Anabel is barking at my side.

I quickly pack snow into a ball and hold it high, throwing it at Nico when he creeps around the bend.

"¡Me atrapaste! (You got me)," he cries, before falling to the ground.

I run over to him, kick snow on his legs and kneel down beside him. The snow here is deep and soft, so I shout, "Snow angels!" and lie with my arms and legs spread wide, moving them in tandem to create the angel design. As Anabel runs off, Nico does the same, and we both jump up to see our work. We say nothing for a moment, and then we hug.

"*Los ángeles nos vigilan* Kate (Angels are watching over us, Kate)," says Nico. "This will be a good winter."

When we get inside, we see that his mother has stocked the kitchen and left a vase of flowers on the dining room table.

"Look," says Nico, "she left us a note." He hands me a pink piece of paper that says, *¡Disfrute!* and I ask him what it means.

"It means enjoy!" he explains as he adjusts the thermostat, which is on the dining room wall. "You'll be warm, soon."

We haven't been to his house in months, but I vividly remember the first time I was there. Maté gourds are still lined up along the colorful kitchen shelves and the stained glass windows cast rainbows on the wood floor. Anabel has found her bed and is lying there, snoring. I shiver, but not because of the cold. I am happy here.

"Let's have a candlelit dinner," I say to Nico while opening cartons on the kitchen counter, "like we did our first night." He turns to me.

"Ah, our first night," he says, narrowing his eyes.

"Or," he adds, "we could skip the candlelight and the dinner." I stare at him and blush. After so many months, I'm still smitten.

Walking over, he takes my hand.

"Follow me," he says, and happily, I do. As he leads me to the bedroom my body tingles with anticipation. I've made love to Nico many times, but tonight it will be different. Tonight he will make love to me.

CHAPTER 13
HEAL

When Clay and I first made love, I hated to be touched. "Kate," he said, "I'm not going to hurt you." Though I knew he wouldn't, his hands felt like weapons. I cringed, nearly crying. Over time, we achieved a tolerable union and eventually I enjoyed him, but I never looked forward to sex. He encouraged me to read or watch pornography, which I hated, and eventually we went to counseling.

"Clearly," surmised the counselor, "this has to do with your mother." I grew weary of hearing that, so eventually we stopped counseling altogether, and I spent more time at work. I knew it wasn't fair to Clay.

"I'm sorry," I would tell him. "I'm trying to feel, truly I am, but I'm not there yet. I just need time."

As Nico removes my clothes, I shiver. We're standing and once again I'm covered with goose bumps. Every cell in my body is jumping for joy.

"Cold?" he asks as he takes off his shirt.

"No," I answer, "it's you."

I touch his face and then his neck as he places his hands on my waist. His scent, a mixture of cologne and sweat, is so intoxicating that I feel weak. He pulls me close and kisses me deeply on the mouth. I begin to wrap my arms around his neck, but he gently pulls me down to the bed and rolls me onto my stomach. Stretching my arms over my head, he straddles and then kisses me, first on my neck, then on my shoulders, and finally down my spine, lightly massaging each vertebra with the tip of his tongue. I'm so aroused that when he kisses me under my arms and alongside my breasts, I moan with pleasure and arch my back. He helps me to kneel and then he enters me. Within moments we climax together and then we collapse. As I roll over, he places a pillow beneath my hips, smiles and slides down the bed below my waist. As he lightly kisses the skin between my thighs, I grip his hair, almost breathless, until his tongue moves inside me. Screaming his name, I climax, and afterward he covers me with the sheet.

Rolling onto his side, he gently strokes my hair. I watch him as he pulls a few loose strands behind my ears; his beard is moist and his eyes are kind. Nico is both strong and tender, and today, as the light of day fades into the dark of night, I feel his love more than ever.

"Thank you, Nico," I whisper, and he kisses me gently on the lips.

"*De nada*," he whispers back. "*¿Todavía tienes hambre?* (Still hungry)." And I laugh.

AFTER SETTLING INTO THE HOUSE, Nico and I adjust to our new wintertime routine. Nearly every day he is gone from 6 a.m. until dark teaching skiing at the resort, and I spend mornings working at my computer. Gus and I correspond nearly every day since I am working on a story about the Argentine economy.

"Holy shit!" he writes when he first reads it. "What a mess!"

He nags me about doing the counterfeit peso story but I dissuade him from pursuing it.

"I heard it's not a big deal," I tell him. "Plus, one Argentina problem at a time, OK?"

At noon I practice yoga before changing into warmer clothes for a walk to town. Each walk takes nearly two hours and ends at the bottom of the hill next to Plaza Mayor. Sometimes I stop in to say hi to Mecha, who is always welcoming and serves me hot cocoa and biscuits. Her homemade breads and cakes are popular in town, and she serves them to her guests each morning for breakfast. She saves the leftovers for me.

One day she decides she will teach me how to bake.

"Your mother never taught you?" she asks with disbelief. When I answer, "No," she hands me an apron and tells me to wash my hands. I think of Princess Diana and Gaiman.

"It's time you learned," she says. "Nico loves cake."

TODAY IS A HOLIDAY IN CHILE, so hundreds of tourists are

in San Martín to ski. The sidewalks are teeming with people wearing brightly colored parkas and snow pants, and many are wearing giant ski goggles that dangle around their necks. Some of the women and girls wear whimsical knit caps designed like cupcakes or animals. One cap looks like a fox, complete with a long fluffy tail, and another has a huge yellow flower sewn to its side. The men's caps are mostly plain and dark except for one that is designed like a giraffe's head. It's cold and windy today, so I decide to stop at one of the town's many chocolate shops to buy a cup of cocoa.

"Kate?" I hear the voice and think it's familiar. When I turn to see who it is, my throat tightens.

"Marina?" I remove my cap and mittens. "How are you?"

She's dressed in a bright pink jacket and blue jeans and is standing at the checkout counter. Her hair is damp and her cheeks are red. I wonder if she's been skiing at the resort. Nico is teaching there today.

"Just a second," she says to the clerk before walking over to me. Extending her hand, she smiles and asks, "How are you?"

I take her hand and smile back; though I haven't seen her for nearly a year, I remember how petite she is. Her hand feels so bony that I'm afraid I'll break it, so I lightly grip her fingers and shake them instead. This feels awkward and I apologize.

"Sorry," I respond, "my hands are cold. Otherwise, I'm good. And you?"

She lowers her head and stomps her boots on the floor. They're covered with dirty snow.

"I'm good. I've been skiing, but I have to be careful. You know, because of my arm."

I resist the urge to ask if she saw Nico, but then she allays my fears.

"How's Nico?" she asks. "I haven't seen him for a while."

Nico never talks about Marina, unless I bring her up. I've done that only once and it was around Christmas, just a few weeks before I caught my big brown trout. We had finished decorating our tree and were sitting at the dining room table addressing envelopes for our Christmas cards, which had "Happy Holidays from Patagonia" printed on the front. Since it was summer and warm, we were drinking ice-cold lemonade and munching on sausage and cheese. "Would you like to send Marina and her family a Christmas card?" I asked him.

Instead of answering right away, he looked up from the table, widened his eyes and slowly nodded his head.

"Don't you think that would be insensitive?" he asked slowly. I blushed.

"Yes, of course," I stammered, "I don't want to hurt her feelings."

Standing up from the table, he walked briskly into the kitchen. This was familiar. During any tension in our relationship, which was rare, he would vanish. Usually I left him alone, but this time I followed. He was washing his lemonade glass in the sink.

"Nico, I'm sorry," I said, standing at the kitchen doorway, "I don't want to cause problems."

Drying the glass, he turned to me.

"Problems?" he asked. "I'm sorry, Kate, that's not the issue. I promised Marina I would help her and now I can't. This isn't your problem. It's mine."

"Nico?" I ask Marina as we stand together in the chocolate shop. "He's fine. He's teaching at Chapelco, as you know."

"No," she answers, "I didn't know. Well, I figured he might since he teaches there every year."

The clerk at the counter coughs to get Marina's attention, so she waves at me.

"I have to leave," she explains, walking away. "It was good to see you. Maybe we'll see each other again sometime?"

"Sure!" I blurt, and quickly seek refuge in an aisle where shelves are stocked with boxes of bonbons. Pretending to be interested, I wait until she leaves the store, and when she does, I relax. I realize that I've been holding my breath.

That night, I tell Nico about seeing Marina. We're lying on the couch facing each other, our heads propped on pillows and our legs intertwined. I'm massaging his feet.

"Yeah?" he asks sleepily. "What did she say?"

"Nothing much," I tell him as I watch him yawn. "Just 'how

are you,' that kind of thing."

Nico smiles and narrows his eyes.

"Did she tell you I haven't seen her for a while?" I pick up my pillow and gently throw it at him.

"Yes," I respond, "that did come up."

Nico and I don't mention Marina again for the rest of the week. I finish my story about the Argentine economy and Gus sends me a short email stating that it has been published.

"Grab your hat!" he writes.

Indeed, the Argentines criticize my work, stating in social media: "*¡La mujer no sabe nada sobre nosotros!* (She knows nothing about us)." Nico tells me to ignore this, but because I want to be accepted, I continue to practice my Spanish with Diego. I rarely speak in Spanish with Nico.

"Too shy to try?" he asks one night as we're waiting in line to be seated at a local restaurant. He pulls me close, musses my hair and kisses me on top of the head.

"I've never known you to be shy, Kate."

"I *am* shy!" I exclaim. When people at a nearby table turn to stare, I whisper in his ear.

"You just don't know me."

"Hmmm," he whispers back, rubbing my bottom. "Yes, I do know you. I know you *veeery* well." The people at the table are still watching us and they smile.

I playfully slap him on the arm as I turn to see a group of people walking through the front door. It's Marina with her brothers, Alex and José, so I grip Nico's jacket.

"It's OK," he whispers in my ear before walking over to greet them. He hugs Marina and shakes her brothers' hands. I can't hear what they're saying but Marina is laughing hard, as if Nico has just told her the funniest joke in the world. My stomach tightens and my eyes burn; I try to look disinterested. I briefly think about what Nidra told me and wonder if Alex or José is involved with the counterfeit pesos. Then Nico takes my hand and leads me to the group.

"Kate, you remember Alex and José? And of course you know Marina." As I shake their hands they say "*Hola*" before turning to Nico. They converse briefly in Spanish and Marina looks at me.

"Let's speak in English for Kate," she says.

"No," says Nico, watching me, "Kate speaks Spanish now. *¿Correcto?*" I swallow hard and remember what Diego taught me.

"*¡Me muero de hambre!* (I'm starving)," I exclaim. Nico smiles and the hostess approaches to tell us that our table is ready. Her timing is perfect and I feel so grateful that I want to hug her. When we sit down, Nico leans over and takes my hand.

"You OK?" he asks. I smile and blush.

"Yes, of course," I respond, "I'm fine." Fortunately, Marina and her brothers have been escorted to another room. I pause before speaking again.

"Nico, Gus wants me to work on a story about counterfeit pesos. He heard that they are being given to U.S. tourists here in exchange for dollars. Do you know anything about that?"

Nico picks up a menu and begins to read. He says nothing for a moment, and then he sets the menu down and looks at me.

"We're always straight with each other, right?" he asks. I nod and he continues.

"I heard about the pesos a long time ago at the weekly *asados* that I used to attend before I met you. One of Marina's brothers is involved. I want you to leave it alone."

I am surprised by his admonition and say nothing for a moment. I don't want to leave it alone.

"Gus says they are taking advantage of U.S. tourists," I finally tell him. "That's not right."

I watch Nico's cheeks turn red and I realize that he's getting angry.

But before he can respond, a small band of male singers approaches our table. It's a motley crew: all are unshaven and one wears a dirty red bandana on his head. Nico rolls his eyes and I can tell that he's getting ready to ask them to leave. But before he can, the man wearing the bandana looks at me and speaks.

"Any requests, miss?" he asks, smiling. I smile back.

"Uh, let me think," I respond, narrowing my eyes. I'm avoiding Nico's glare. "Do you know any American songs?" The man vigorously nods his head and begins to tune his guitar.

"We do a good rendition of Neil Diamond's 'Sweet Caroline.' Will that do?"

I laugh. I love Neil Diamond.

"Yes!" I exclaim, clapping my hands. "Please!"

I look at Nico, wink and mouth, "I love you." He winks back.

It seems as if everyone in the restaurant knows the lyrics to "Sweet Caroline" because we happily sing the chorus together. Out of the corner of my eye I see Marina and her brothers as they peer into our room; they appear to be singing, too. At the end of the song, we all cheer and applaud as the band moves to the next table.

I lean toward Nico and apologize for interrupting our conversation.

"No problem," he responds, "it was fun to sing. But there's still the issue with the pesos. It's not what you or Gus thinks. Marina's brother is a good man. He spent time in Buenos Aires where the ring is operating and they approached him to distribute the money here. He refused and they went after him. It was very bad. He lives here now and I want you to leave it alone. Please."

I look down at my menu and my cheeks get warm. The journalist in me is resisting but I don't want to cause any more problems for Marina or her family. I wonder why Nico is taking their side and not mine.

"OK," I say, reluctantly. "I'll tell Gus that I don't want to do the story."

He reaches across the table and takes my hand.

"Thank you, Kate. People in Argentina do what they can to survive. We don't always have choices like you do in the U.S."

I look at him and smile but my throat tightens. He still considers me a foreigner. I begin to worry.

"I don't understand, Nico. What do you mean?"

"I mean that our pesos are worth less and less each day. Your dollars are more secure. Most of us here go along with that but some resent it. People from the U.S. can go home and get more dollars. It's not so easy for us."

I pull my hand away and stare at the menu, but what I really want to do is run and hide. My worry is replaced by fear. Does Nico resent me, too?

After ordering, he folds his arms on the table and leans toward me.

"Kate, I'm glad to be with you. Why, exactly, are you with me?"

I look at him, surprised. He's asking now? I wonder if it's because he's seen Marina or because we've just argued. I stare at him for a few seconds and suddenly feel warm. His head is slightly tilted and his beautiful green eyes are watching me. He is so handsome, so sexy, that my fear is quickly replaced by lust and love. I smile as I consider my answer and my eyes fill with tears.

When my father was alive, I asked him about my future husband. I was six years old.

"Daddy?" I asked, pushing Pink Lace in her stroller. We were at our vacation home and he was cleaning fishing rods in his shed. "Will I marry someone like you?"

He smiled, looked at me and dipped his rag into a small pot of wax.

"I hope not, baby," he said, smiling. "You should marry someone far more handsome!"

I stopped the stroller and picked up Pink Lace, cradling her in my arms.

"Daaaaddy!" I said, laughing. "I'm serious!"

Setting down his rag, he turned and looked at me.

"OK," he said, "you should marry someone who respects you, is kind and makes you laugh. It should be someone who accepts you for who you are, who never wants to change you and who makes you feel good about yourself all the time. I know that he's out there somewhere, you'll see."

As the server delivers our food, I wipe my eyes with my napkin. Nico is still watching me.

"Aside from the great sex?" I ask and he smiles before I continue.

"Baby, I'm with you for a hundred reasons, but mostly because you're strong and kind, and you accept me for who I am."

He nods his head and leans back.

"And why," I ask, "are you with me?"

He picks up his fork and grins.

"Because of the great sex," he says, and I laugh.

CHAPTER 14
TRUST

It's early morning and Nico and I are in bed naked, a thick down comforter pulled to our necks. On most days we like to awaken slowly, but today Nico briskly informs me that he's heading to Bolivia tomorrow to work as a fishing guide in the jungle. A friend asked him yesterday to fill in for a guide there who got sick. He'll be gone for two months. I sit up and stare at him.

"What? Bolivia? The Amazon? Now? What about skiing?"

He pulls me down and embraces me so that I can't move. Then he kisses my head.

"Dorado, Kate," he explains, "golden dorado. They're enormous – real fighters, and they live in the jungle. They can grow up to 50 pounds. There are other fish, too, like pacu. And the natives there are very primitive. They fish in wood canoes and use bows and arrows to hunt for their food. There's a lodge that's very popular there and they need me to guide."

I say nothing for a moment, imagining him in the jungle with giant insects, reptiles and roaming carnivores, not to mention malaria. And what was that fish with the funny name that he mentioned? I'd never heard of it. Is it like a piranha? Does it bite?

I worry that he won't be safe; plus, I won't see him for two months. I want to leap from the bed to object, but since his body feels so warm, I simply snuggle closer and sigh.

"You have to go?" I ask, trying to turn my head to look at him.

"*Confía en mí en esto* (Trust me on this)," he says, pulling me closer. "I have to do it."

It's not easy being in love with fishermen. Though they may love you, they mostly love to fish. And because they're sportsmen, they usually prefer the outdoors and may chafe at being confined. Nico is like that.

"*Quiero ir contigo* (I want to go with you)," I say, wistfully, into the pillow.

"Not this time," he answers, leaping from the bed. "I'll take you on a trip another time."

That night while packing he tells me it would be best if I moved to my house to be closer to Nidra and Fede.

"They're staying at Hermosas Montañas this winter," he explains as he stuffs a pile of khaki pants into his duffel. "They'll watch out for you. I don't want you to be alone here, even though Anabel is with you. If there's a lot of snow, it will be hard to get down the driveway."

I nod my head but don't speak. I'm feeling sorry for myself and he knows it.

"It's only two months, Kate," he says, walking over to me. He puts his arms around my head and pulls me close to his chest. His hugs are therapeutic and erotic, but tonight I don't feel like making love. Instead, I feel like crying.

He moves back and gently lifts my chin to look at me.

"Do you know what the Spanish word *pucheros* means, Kate?" he asks. I don't, but nod my head. "It means pouting and that's what you're doing. Sometimes we have to make decisions that we don't like and that's what I'm doing now. We could use the money, so it will be for the best. Trust me."

I smile at him and nod.

The next morning as he loads his gear in the truck, I try not to cry. It's cold outside and snowing, and the sky, full of clouds, is gray. Anabel is sitting next to me, watching us.

"Wish I could go, too," I tell her, rubbing her head.

When Nico finishes, he shuts the hatch and strides over to me, his hands tucked in his pockets. He explains that he'll first catch a plane at Chapelco Airport to fly to Santa Cruz de la Sierra in eastern Bolivia before catching a smaller plane to fly to the lodge, which sits near the river in the rain forest.

"Keep in touch, OK?" I ask, folding my arms and hugging them tight against my chest.

He smiles and scans the ground before picking up a rock. It's brown with pink lines.

"Remember this?" he asks, rubbing it clean on his shirt before handing it to me. "When you hold this rock, think of me." I smile, throw my arms around his neck and kiss him.

"I will," I say, tears welling in my eyes. "I promise I will."

As I watch him drive away, I wonder what to do next. Anabel, who has followed Nico to the end of the driveway, runs up to me and barks as if suggesting a plan.

"OK girl," I say, rubbing her neck, "give me a few minutes to change clothes and we'll go for a walk, OK?"

Turning toward the house, I wonder if I can call Eva. Since it's 7 a.m. in Chicago, I figure she's sleeping, but I don't care. After the fifth ring, she answers.

"Hello?" she asks. I burst into tears.

"He's gone," I cry, "to Bolivia."

I wait for her to answer and hear Jason speak in the background.

"Is everything OK?" he asks.

"Just a sec," says Eva into the phone before covering the mouthpiece to speak to Jason. When she comes back, I hear her walking. I imagine she's headed for her kitchen to make coffee.

"Honey," she finally says, "I'm half awake. Did you say Bolivia?"

I smile and wipe my nose with my sleeve, remembering that Eva loves to sleep.

"Yes," I answer, "to fish. He has a gig there for two months."

There's silence for a moment and then she laughs.

"Well, welcome to life with a fishing guide!" I pull the phone away from my ear and flick it with my finger. When I put it back on my ear, I hear her add, "Why don't you come home?" I pause for a second before answering.

"*Esta es mi casa ahora* (This is my home now)," I say, and I stop. Did I just speak to her in Spanish? There's silence on the other end of the line and I wonder if she's hung up, but she hasn't.

"Yes, my dear Kate," she finally says, "I can hear that it is."

Nico asked me one night at dinner if I missed the U.S. We were eating pickled deer and sweet potatoes, our favorite meal.

"No," I answered. "Not at all."

He smiled and took another bite of sweet potato. I loved that he ate with his fork in his left hand, European style. I was doing that now, too.

"You know," he added, chewing. "The other guides here are jealous of me. They wish that they could be with you."

"Sorry?" I asked, setting my fork on my plate. "Jealous? Me?"

He smiled, narrowed his eyes and began to sip his wine, a nice Malbec that his mother gave us. She bought it in Mendoza.

"Foreign women here are exotic," he said, "like Argentine women are in your country." I rolled my eyes and laughed.

"Exotic? Obviously, they don't really know me. Are they nice about it?"

Nico stopped sipping his wine and set down his glass.

"We all get along," he explained. "We are friendly yet we are competitive. Friendships are important in our culture. Are they important in the U.S.?"

I stopped to think. What did he mean by friendships? I had always been a loner, especially since my parents died. I was afraid to get close to anyone and only trusted myself. For a moment, I didn't know how to respond. He asked again.

"Friendships, relationships, Kate, you know, extended families, are they important to you?"

I picked up my napkin, wiped my mouth and changed the subject.

"Is it OK if we talk about something else?" I asked, standing from the table to clear the dishes. "Like what you would like for dessert?"

I stay on the phone and listen while Eva makes coffee. I envision her kitchen with its granite countertops and stainless steel stovetop and refrigerator. My stovetop is made of porcelain and is chipped. My life in Chicago was so much different than my life now, but I tell Eva I wouldn't trade it for anything.

"Fine," she answers. I hear her Keurig as it squeezes coffee into her mug. "But why Bolivia? The mosquitoes there must be the size of bats. Is he crazy?"

I laugh for the first time since Nico told me he was leaving.

"No, he fishes. Apparently there are humongous fish that look like they're made of gold, and it's like heaven there. He's guiding and I'm happy for him. I'm just not happy for me."

There's silence on the other end of the line and I imagine that Eva's thinking of a comeback.

"Clearly, you're in love," she says instead, "but more

importantly, you're beginning to settle down."

Eva and I talk for several minutes before hanging up and I hurry to the bedroom to change into my walking clothes. Anabel is barking outside and I peek out the window to see what's exciting her. A truck is parked in the driveway; since it's not familiar, I reach for my robe.

"Why so early?" I wonder. I pull on my robe and grab my jacket to walk outside. When I open the door, I see José, Marina's brother, walking up the driveway. He smiles at me before speaking.

"*¡Hola!* Is Nico home?" I put on my jacket and walk outside. This is odd, I think.

"No," I answer, closing the door. "He just left for Bolivia; he'll be gone for two months. Is something wrong?"

José stops walking and starts to turn back toward the truck. Pausing, he turns around and speaks.

"It's Marina," he says. "She can't move her arm at all. We don't know what to do, and I was hoping that Nico could help."

I say nothing for a second before gesturing for him to come inside. Why is he asking for Nico's help? Why isn't he calling the doctor in town?

José follows me into the living room with Anabel close behind and I close the door.

"I don't understand," I say. "Is Marina sick? Did you call the doctor?"

José wipes his feet on the rug near the door before answering. I can tell that he's nervous.

"The doctor says there's nothing that we can do except rehab," he explains. "The nerves in her arm are nearly dead. She's asking for Nico to see if he can help her."

I stare at him; I feel sorry for Marina but don't understand why she needs Nico's help. What is going on? Does Nico still see her? Are they involved? What have I been missing? A tsunami of hurt washes over me, and my body feels numb. I trust Nico; am I wrong?

José, as if sensing my angst, puts his hands up with his palms facing me.

"Don't worry," he says rapidly, "this isn't about their relationship. It's just that Nico knows the therapist who helped her and since he always drove her there, Marina asked me to get directions." I feel myself begin to breathe.

"Oh," I say, "I understand, it's OK. We can send Nico a text message. I'm sure he will help."

We stare at each other for a moment before he speaks.

"You know," he says quietly, "she doesn't blame you."

I feel myself blush. So they do talk about it. And what do they say? Do they gossip that I stole Nico away and that I'm evil? Do I tell José what I think, which is that I feel I've betrayed Marina and never want to see her again? Do I reach out to him to soothe his worry and reassure him that his sister will be OK? Not knowing what else to do, I ask him if he would like some coffee.

"Yes," he answers, following me into the kitchen, "that would be nice."

I learn that day that José is also a fisherman and that he guides for a lodge near town.

"Nico and I fished together as kids," he informs me as he drinks his coffee. He's handsome; his short dark hair, once damp from the falling snow, has dried, and his long legs, peeking out from beneath the table, are crossed at the ankles.

He seems at ease with me and I'm beginning to like him.

"Tell me about Marina's arm," I coax. "How can I help?"

Even as I say this, I'm wondering if I mean it, but before I can take it back, José speaks.

"Thank you for asking," he says. "Actually it would help if you could talk to her. I want her to learn how to fish."

I remembered what Marina said at the *asado* so many months ago: "I don't like to fish."

I stare at José before speaking.

"Now?" I ask, swallowing hard. He smiles and nods his head.

"Not right now, but soon perhaps, just to cast. I think it will strengthen her arm." He drains his coffee cup and stands to walk to the counter.

"You're a woman and a role model," he says, "she doesn't like to take orders from me."

I nod my head as if agreeing, but instead I'm feeling sick. I'm thinking to myself that this is so odd. Doesn't she hate me?

I look at José. I can't say no. I've already hurt her.

"OK," I say, walking to the sink to wash my cup, "I'm happy to help. When do you want to get started?"

CHAPTER 15
FORGIVE

As Nico requested, I move back to my house a few days after he leaves. It's early evening and I don't want to be alone since I can't stop thinking about Marina.

I wonder if Diego is home. When I knock on his door, he opens it just a crack.

"*¡Hola!*" he answers, peeking through the crack. He doesn't invite me in. That's odd, I think, until I hear a woman's voice.

"*¿Quién está ahí,* Diego? (Who's there, Diego)," she yells. He blushes.

"*Es mi madre* (It's my mother)," he says to me. "*¡Hoy es mi cumpleaños!* (Today is my birthday)."

I lean over and touch his fingers, which are gripping the door.

"*¡Feliz cumpleaños!* (Happy birthday)," I tell him.

The door swings open. A small woman with white curly hair steps out. She's the same size as Diego and has his same smile, and she's wearing an embroidered white shirt and blue jeans.

"*¿Eres Kate?* (Is this Kate)," she asks, and I grin.

"*Sí,*" I respond. "*Soy* Kate (Yes, I am Kate)."

When will you stop hiding who you are?" asked Eva one day while we were having lunch at Nordstrom. We were both eating the salmon salad, our favorite.

"What do you mean," I asked with my mouth full. I sipped my iced tea while waiting for her to respond.

"You know, everything that went on with your mom and stuff. You should bring it out and tell people about it. It will help you and it will help other kids whose parents are monsters." I shake my head.

"My mother wasn't a monster, she just missed my dad," I said as I buttered a slice of bread. "And I'm fine with it."

Eva stared at me for a second before responding.

"No you're not," she said. "You barely talk about yourself at all with other people. I've watched you. Being at a dinner party with you is like being by myself. All we talk about is me and afterward, people can barely remember your name."

I knew she was right. I still hid my past from others. I never felt comfortable talking about myself. What if something slipped out?

Diego finally invites me in and formally introduces us.

"*Su nombre es* Rosario (Her name is Rosario)," he explains. She takes my hand.

"It's OK, Kate," she says with a thick accent, "we can speak in English. It will help me to practice. OK?" I nod my head and smile before giving a thumbs-up signal to Diego. He shrugs his shoulders and heads to the kitchen.

"We're having a very small dinner since his party is tomorrow," she says, "would you like to join us?"

I nod my head, smile and follow her to the kitchen. The dining table is littered with small glass bowls half full of food. A single cupcake with white icing sits in the middle, an unlit candle poked in its top. Rosario laughs.

"Diego is not one year old as you know," she says, "but sometimes he acts like it! Please, sit down."

Diego rushes over and pulls out my chair. The kitchen is warm and smells sweet with the aroma of cooking food, so after I sit I close my eyes to enjoy it.

Diego, hovering and holding a dish of meat, breaks his vow of speaking to me only in Spanish.

"Kate, would you like some lamb?" he asks.

"Yes, I would, thank you."

When he finally sits down, Rosario offers a prayer.

"Dear Lord," she says, "thank you for our food and for bringing us Kate, amen." Diego and I laugh.

"A condensed prayer," he says, but my eyes are stinging with tears. I pick up my fork and knife.

"Kate," asks Rosario, "Diego tells me that you live next door with Nico. Is he guiding now?"

I wipe my eyes with my napkin and smile.

"Yes," I tell her, "he's in Bolivia, catching golden dorado."

Diego, who has been eating ravenously, looks up from his plate.

"*¡Ninguna mierda!* (No shit)," he cries, and immediately covers his head with his hands. Rosario hits him in the arm with her fork.

I mouth "*un tenedor*" to him and smile.

"I mean," he adds, rubbing his arm, "that's incredible! The Amazon!" I nod my head.

"Yes," I continue, "he left a few days ago. He'll be back in two months."

Diego, still chewing, asks me if I'm speaking in Spanish to Nico yet.

"*¡Sí!*" I exclaim, then for Rosario's benefit, add, "Your son has taught me well. I finally feel comfortable speaking in your language."

She watches me but says nothing. We eat for a few minutes before she speaks.

"Please tell me about your family, Kate. Where do your parents live?"

I feel myself get tense and grip my fork.

"My parents are both gone," I answer. "My father died when I was 12 years old."

"Oh, I am sorry," she says. "Tell us what happened."

I explain that my father loved to fish, had died suddenly of a heart attack and that my mother died as a result of alcoholism. Because Rosario and Diego listen intently I don't stop talking until I'm finished eating. Suddenly, talking about my past feels cathartic, and tonight it doesn't bother me to share. Instead of feeling judged, I feel embraced.

After dinner we decide to eat dessert in the living room, so I help Diego clear the plates before I leave the kitchen. When I sit on the sofa, I look around and my eyes rest on an open amethyst geode, its deep violet quartz reflecting the shimmering light of a nearby candle. The effect is hypnotizing. When Rosario walks in, I jump up to help her with dessert. She's divided the cupcake into three pieces and each piece is on a separate plate along with a scoop of vanilla ice cream. The plates are neatly arranged on a tray along with three spoons and bright orange napkins. I take the tray from her and set it on a table near the couch while Diego comes in with a pot of coffee and mugs. She sits in a nearby chair.

As we eat, Rosario tells me about her family. I'm surprised to hear that she has six daughters and that all are older than Diego. Her husband, she explains, died last year.

"Cancer," she says, slowly nodding her head. "It was awful."

Then she asks me about Nico. I tell her we're happy.

"He's a nice man," she says. "I hear from Julieta that you'll be helping Marina with her arm."

I carefully set my fork on my dessert plate and stare at her for a moment before speaking. I think to myself that San Martín is such a small town.

"Yes," I say, my throat tight, "that is correct. José, her brother, asked me to teach her how to fly cast." Rosario smiles at me and leans forward.

"When my husband got sick, I thought a lot about life," she says, "and how it's so short."

Diego, who has been quiet most of the evening, stands from the couch and asks me if I want more coffee. I tell him yes and he takes my cup before walking to the kitchen. Rosario smiles at him and continues.

"I also realized that life could be, how do you say it? Difficult, and that everyone has to cope with something hard. Like your mother had to cope after your father died."

My eyes begin to burn and I try not to cry. Rosario moves to sit with me on the sofa and takes my hand.

"Before he died, my husband made me promise that I would always be kind. He suffered so much that he never wanted anyone to suffer at all." She squeezes my hand. "I think that you, my dear Kate, feel the same."

The tears I was holding back cascade down my face and she hands me a napkin. Instead of wiping my eyes, I reach into my pocket and feel the rock that Nico gave me before he left. I carry it everywhere.

"It's right for you to help Marina," says Rosario, "because by helping her, you help Nico, too. Most of all, you help yourself."

When Diego returns with coffee, he stops in the middle of the room, sets my cup on the table, and sits next to me.

"What happened?" he asks, wrapping his arm around my shoulders. "Why are you crying?" Rosario smiles.

"Kate *es una buena mujer* (Kate is a good woman)," she says.

I nod my head to indicate that I understand.

MARINA LIVES IN A LARGE HOUSE near the ski resort. As I drive there the next day to give her casting lessons, I feel anxious.

"It's OK with me," said Nico when I sent him a text to tell him about it. "You're great to help her, but I know you'll feel uncomfortable."

I smile now, remembering what he said. The word uncomfortable seems mild.

I pull into her driveway by 10 a.m. The sky is clear and the bright sun reflects off newly fallen snow. I reach into the console, pull out my sunglasses and put them on. I look around and wonder if this is a good idea. As I consider whether I should turn back, I see Marina standing at the window. She waves. José must have told her that I was coming.

"Great," I whisper as I turn off the engine. "Eva would love this." I open the door but the wind blows it shut so I reopen it with my foot and grab my fishing bag from the seat. Inside the bag are a four-piece fishing rod, a reel, line, tippet, and a few flies that I bought in town.

"*¡Hola!*" says Marina as she opens the door. "*¡Buenos dias!*"

"Good morning!" I respond, smiling. "Good to see you!"

She holds the door open as I walk through.

"Please, make yourself at home. José told me you were coming."

I enter her home and stop in a small foyer next to her living room, which is full of large furniture. The walls are covered with paintings, portraits and group photographs, and I'm reminded of Julieta's home. Ah yes, I think, family. It's so important here.

I set my bag on the floor and look at Marina. Her skin is pale and she seems thinner than ever. Her injured arm is in a sling and she gestures to the kitchen with her other hand.

"Coffee?" she asks. "I just put some on. Or would you prefer maté?" I smile at the suggestion.

"Coffee," I respond, and she nods.

She gestures to me that we should walk to the kitchen.

"José tells me that I should learn how to fly-fish," she says as she pulls two large red coffee mugs from the cabinet. "But, as you know, I don't like to fish."

"I understand," I say, "but it grows on you after a while." She shakes her head.

"I don't think it will grow on me, but he's convinced that the casting will help my arm. I told him I would try it." She grins at me before turning to the kitchen table. "Here," she adds, "please sit down and show me what you have in your fishing bag."

As a child, I used to love my father's fishing bag, which was always full of treasures.

"See if you can find the reel," he said to me one day when I was digging through it. I was five years old. "Close your eyes and you should be able to feel it. It's metal and round."

When I finally found it, I pulled it out and turned the handle to watch it spin.

"Now," he said, "see you if you can find the rod."

I reached inside again and felt what seemed like several narrow sticks held together by a wide rubber band.

"This?" I asked him, pulling them out.

"Yep," he said, smiling, "that's my girl. You're very smart. Now, someday I'll teach you how to fish."

Today, I explain my fishing bag contents to Marina.

"Here's the reel," I explain, pulling it out and setting it on the table.

"And here," I add, removing a long roll of cloth tied at one end, "is the rod bag. The rod is inside, in four pieces. I also brought line and a few flies. You know what those are, right?"

When she doesn't answer, I look at her. The color has fully drained from her face. I wonder if she's going to faint.

"Did Nico tie those?" she asks, and I quickly shake my head.

"No," I tell her, "I bought them in town."

"What else is in there?" she asks with a tight smile.

Feeling around on the bottom, my fingers graze the rock that Nico gave me before he left. I push it aside and pull out a small plastic pouch that holds a long strand of 6-weight tippet.

"This is tippet and you attach the fly on one end," I explain. "I'll tie on the fly for you, and then I'll show you how to cast."

I don't realize how nervous I am until I assemble the rod. Marina is silent, watching me, and my palms are sweating, making it difficult to tighten together each piece of the rod. My hands shake as I add the reel, and only after I tighten the ring that holds it to the rod do I realize that I've put it on backward.

"Ha," I laugh, looking at Marina, "I do this wrong all the time." Unscrewing the ring, I flip the reel so the line will feed correctly down the shaft of the rod. My hands are still shaking.

Marina is looking at the flies that are lying on the table, poking them with the finger of her free hand.

"They're beautiful," she says, "works of art, every one of them. Nico learned how to tie when he was a child. I used to watch him."

I swallow hard, wishing I wasn't there. A quick casting lesson, I think, and then I'm gone.

"You know," she adds after a few seconds, "I never saw him happier than when he met you."

Stunned, I stop working and set down the rod.

"Marina," I say, "I'm not here to talk about Nico. I'm here only because José asked me to help you."

Smiling, she shakes her head.

"I know," she says. "I'm sorry. It's just that you and I have this thing between us, like a wide raging river that I need to cross to feel safe on the other side."

I watch her as she speaks, wondering where this is going.

"I've thought about this a lot," she continues, "and I want you and me to be friends. Nico would want that. Is that possible?"

I sit in the chair next to her and take a deep breath.

"Sure," I tell her, "we can be friends, but first let's start with being fishing buddies, OK? Have you ever cast a fishing rod?"

After the rod is assembled, we put on our coats, gloves and sunglasses and walk outside. Behind the house is a small pond that is frozen now, but I figure we can pretend it's full of fish. I turn to Marina.

"Ten and two," I explain as I strip line from the reel, "I'll demonstrate. Try to get it off shore a few yards."

Whipping the rod back, I force it forward.

"Remember," I shout, "power in the back cast!" The fly drops lightly to the ice.

"And," I add, demonstrating, "always hold the rod tip up!"

Marina is smiling. Her free hand is extended along the top of her sunglasses, further protecting her eyes from the sun.

"OK," she responds, "let me try it!"

I hand her the rod and watch as she adjusts her sling. For a moment I feel protective, but recognize that she doesn't need protection. Instead, I realize, she deserves my respect. Having lost Nico to me, she still graciously welcomes me into her home and is attempting to cast a fishing line, even though she doesn't like to fish.

I smile. I want Nico to see this, so I pull out my phone, take Marina's picture, and send it to him.

WEEKS PASS and I continue to visit Marina to teach her how

to fly-fish. We never mention Nico again and instead are getting to know one another as friends.

One day I showed Marina's photo to Diego.

"*¡Eso es increíble!* (That is amazing)," he said. "*¡Eres una buena persona!* (You're a good person)."

Gus, however, felt differently.

"Are you nuts?" he shouted when I told him what I was doing. "Are you sure she's not after Nico?" I rolled my eyes before I responded.

"Maybe, but I think Nico and I are strong enough now so that won't happen."

After I hung up, I sat down and wondered. Was Gus correct? Is that what was going on?

TODAY DURING OUR CASTING LESSON, Marina removes her sling and places the rod handle in the palm of her disabled hand, using her other hand to curl her fingers around it.

"Kate," she says, adjusting the rod, "there's some masking tape in the kitchen in the drawer next to the sink. Would you mind getting it for me? I can secure the rod in my hand with it."

I run into the house and find the tape, and when I run back out I see José pull into the driveway.

"Whoa!" he calls to Marina as he leaves the truck, slamming the door. "*¿Estás sujetando una caña de pescar?* (Are you holding a fishing rod)."

I smile and stop, watching as he walks over to her and places his hand gently on her cheek. He leans over, kisses her head, steps back, and looks at me.

"Kate!" he shouts. "*¡Te quiero!* (I love you)." I laugh and walk over to them, tape in hand. Together, José and I wrap the tape around Marina's hand, and though the rod wobbles, it stays in place as she holds it with her other hand to cast.

"Ten and two!" she cries, as the rod moves high and then drops low. Unfazed, she tries again.

"Ten and two! Rod tip *up*!"

When the rod stops a little higher, José and I clap. I can tell that Marina is getting tired and I suggest that she stop.

"No," she says, "*gracias*, but I'm going to keep trying."

AT THE END OF AUGUST, Nico tells me that he's coming home. He's been happy in Bolivia, having caught dozens of fish, but he claims in a text message that he's happiest that Marina and I are now friends.

"Takes the pressure off me," I read as I'm sitting outside. The days are getting warmer. "Just kidding," he adds, "I'm happy for both of you."

Smiling, I wait for more, and a smiley face pops up on the screen.

"But I'm mostly happy for me." Laughing, I type back.

"*¡Eres gracioso!* (You are funny)." And then add how much I miss him. "*¡No puedo esperar a verte!* (I cannot wait to see you)." I wait to read his response.

"Sorry," he types, "clients are here. I have to leave now. See you soon!"

I turn off my phone and lean back in the chair. What now? I wonder. Should we invite Marina and her family over for dinner? Will we fish together? Will Nico decide that he loves her again?

I rise from the chair to walk. Anabel, who has been running around barking up the trees, joins me.

"It's just you and me, girl," I tell her, rubbing her head. "Let's get outta here."

We walk for nearly two hours and see a variety of plants, birds and animals, including two wild boars. Anabel chases them off. On the way home, we stop to see Nidra and Fede, who are feeding their horses.

"Howdy, stranger!" shouts Nidra. I haven't seen her since I started giving Marina casting lessons. "Where have you been? We heard that Nico's in Bolivia. We thought you went with him!" I shake my head as I reach out to hug her.

"Nope," I say, "he went alone. But he's coming home in three days." She pulls back to look at me and gasps. "You've lost so much weight, are you OK? You should have dinner with us; let's go inside."

As I follow Nidra I realize that she's right. I haven't been eating much. My nights are being spent at my computer writing about Argentina for Gus. My days are spent helping Marina.

Eva called me one night after Gus told her that I was teaching Marina how to fly cast.

"Katie," she scolded, "what, exactly, is going on there?"

I started to defend myself but stopped.

"Nothing," I said firmly. "She has a disability and I'm helping her to get strong. That's all."

I felt my face get warm and realized I was angry that Gus was talking about me behind my back. "Note to self," I thought, "give him hell."

To Eva, I said, "And why are you concerned?"

Eva didn't waste a breath before responding.

"What if she's taking advantage of you? You know how people can be. Maybe she figures this is a way to get to Nico!"

I paused for a few seconds before answering.

"Kate, are you there?" she asked.

"Yes," I finally said, "things are different here. Relationships are important. We don't just toss people away."

I stopped and suddenly thought of Andrew. I had only spoken to him once since leaving Chicago.

"I can handle it if Nico wants to get back with Marina," I said. "I just want him to be happy. But that's not going to happen. It's just not going to happen." Eva laughed.

"So you fancy yourself as an Argentine now, right?" she asked, her tone sounding mean. "Seriously, Katie," she added, "just be careful."

When Nidra and I enter the lodge, she leads me to the kitchen. She removes cold chicken piccata and pasta from the refrigerator and pulls plates from the cabinet.

"Let's get some food in you," she says, opening the silverware drawer.

While she's working, I tell her about Marina and she turns to look at me.

"Casting lessons?" she asks. "Now that's kind of you. Does Nico know?"

She hands me a piece of chicken. I put it in my mouth, nod at her and wink.

"*Sí, mi amiga* (Yes, my friend)," I say, chewing, "he seems to approve."

Nidra moves to the sink and turns on the water. She removes a glass from the cabinet and fills it.

"Honestly," she says, "things are so much different here."

I smile, nod my head and take another piece of chicken.

"In my experience," she continues, "most women who have been in love with the same man never become friends. Here, it's all about nourishing relationships. You know: honor, good will, *asados*, passing maté, that sort of thing. Looks like you're doing it, too."

I see a roll of paper towels on the counter, remove a sheet and wipe my hands before answering.

"I like Marina," I tell her. "And she's making progress with her arm, too. Whatever happens with Nico will happen with Nico. But I have to trust him. We'll see."

Nidra stares at me for a moment before speaking.

"I presume you never did anything about the counterfeit pesos story?"

I wipe my hands again and nod.

"That is correct," I respond as I toss the towel into the trashcan. "I want to protect my relationship with Nico, not destroy it."

When Anabel and I finally walk home, it's late. The sun is setting and there are glorious reds and oranges painting the sky. Surefooted and happy, I scan the landscape until a sound in the distance catches my attention. I look ahead and see Nico's truck.

"He's home!" I call to Anabel as we begin to run. He's at least a half-mile away and headed toward us, flashing his headlights. When he finally stops, he jumps from the truck, runs to me and picks me up. Twirling me around, he kisses my head, then my face and then my mouth. He tastes sweet, like he's been eating chocolate. When he speaks, I once again feel his deep mellow voice vibrate to my soul.

"Kate! Found you! Missed you! Love you! Now let's go home."

CHAPTER 16
GROW

In October, Nico tells me we're taking a trip.

"Where?" I ask as I turn off my computer after a morning's worth of writing. He's just returned home after getting his truck serviced in town and is carrying a plastic bag. He opens it and pulls out a new Nikon camera.

"Calafate," he answers, peeling off his jacket and tossing it onto a nearby chair, "Perito Moreno, I thought you might like to see it."

I jump up and stare at him.

"Glacier!" I squeal. "Seriously? Now?" I've read that Perito Moreno is the most famous glacier in the Los Glaciares National Park and is fed by the Southern Patagonian Ice Field, the world's second largest contiguous extrapolar ice field. I've seen pictures online and have wanted to see it for months.

Nico's walking briskly to the bedroom and responds in a loud voice.

"Yes, now, let's pack!"

When Nico arrived home from Bolivia, we agreed not to talk about Marina.

"Just let it go," he said as he was unpacking. "It sounds like her arm is getting better. Thank you for helping her."

"OK," I said, smiling as I gathered his clothes to wash them. "How about we talk about us then?"

He stopped unpacking and looked at me.

"Ooookaaaay," he said, suspiciously, "what would you like to talk about?"

I dropped his clothes on the floor and walked toward him, unbuttoning my shirt.

"Let's start with unpacking," I suggested, "and how that can wait."

Calafate is in the southwest part of Argentina's Santa Cruz Province, at least a two-hour flight from San Martín. Nico's father drives us to Chapelco Airport in his old Toyota Highlander and since he doesn't speak English, he simply smiles at me during the ride. Now more confident with my Spanish, I approach him when we arrive at the airport as he's unloading our bags from the back of the truck.

"*¡Emocionados de ver el glaciar!* (Excited to see the glacier)," I say. His face lights up.

"*¡Sí, me han dicho que es maravilloso!* (Yes, I have been told that it's wonderful)," he responds before hugging me. I reach over to Nico and grip his arm.

"Did you hear that?" I exclaim. "Spanish, me and your dad!"

We arrive at the Calafate airport in the late afternoon and rent a small Chevrolet Cavalier from Hertz.

"It's either that or a four-wheel drive truck," explains Nico as he's filling out our paperwork. "Not a lot of choices here."

I smile and scan the terminal, which is small. On the wall outside the baggage area is a giant map of the area, and the Hertz agent asks us where we need to go.

"Estancia Alicia," Nico tells him. "It's about 45 minutes from here."

We pack our bags into the car and climb in. After fastening our seat belts, Nico leans over and kisses me.

"This is for you," he says, smiling, "for helping Marina."

My eyes fill with tears. Have I told him lately that I would do anything for him and that I would follow him to the ends of the earth and beyond? Does he know that my love for him is boundless and that he's helped me to become stronger, more confident and to finally know who I am?

I decide not to tell him now since we're sitting in the airport parking lot. Instead, I simply smile.

"You are welcome, Nico," I say, rubbing his thigh. "I am glad that I could help."

We arrive at Estancia Alicia, a 165,000-acre sheep farm, an hour later. Its lodge is bright yellow with pink flowers along its sidewalk. When we pull up to it, a handsome man with a burgundy tam swiftly walks out the front door to greet us.

"¡Hola!" he shouts. "Are you Nico and Kate?" Nico walks to him and shakes his hand. They chat for a moment before returning to the car to retrieve our bags. The man's name is Jorge, and he manages the lodge along with his wife Lucia, who greets us when we get inside. From her accent, I imagine that she's German.

"Hello," she says warmly, shaking my hand. "Your room is down the hall. When you get settled, please join us in the living room for wine."

Our room is beautiful, with flowered wallpaper and a large ornate washbowl and pitcher set on a pink doily in the center of our dresser. Enchanted by this feminine décor, I decide to tease Nico, who's setting our bags near the closet.

"I guess that's where you'll be washing your face," I say, pointing to the bowl.

But instead of smiling, he grabs me.

"Tell you what," he says, wrapping his arms around my waist. His hands rest on my bottom. "How about we skip the wine in the living room and have our own tasting here?"

I nod my head and gently kiss his mouth, slowly moving my tongue along the inside of his lips. "Perfect white teeth," I whisper, remembering the first time I saw him. I feel his excitement and my body responds, tingling like it did when our hands first touched. I reach down, unzip my pants and push them to the floor along with my panties. He moves the washbowl, pitcher and doily onto the bed and lifts me onto the dresser. He tenderly kisses my breasts, and when I lean back and groan, he moves lower to kiss my thighs. As he moves his tongue inside me, I grip his hair. My orgasm is swift and strong.

Afterward I watch, dreamily, as he picks me up and sets me on the bed. I lie back, watch him undress and pull him close when he enters me. His orgasm, like mine, happens quickly, and when we hear a knock on the door, he covers my mouth with his hand. I'm trying hard not to laugh.

"Just a minute!" he yells at the door. "I'm washing my face!"

AT DINNER Lucia tells us about Calafate.

"The city is named after the calafate bush, which has yellow flowers and dark blue berries. It's very common here."

Nico is eating and watching me, occasionally catching my eye and pretending to wash his face.

"Funny," I mouth to him as I try to pay attention to Lucia.

"Tomorrow you'll see the glacier," she adds. "It's amazing, really." We're eating salmon, which is sitting in foil and covered with white sauce and capers; Nico doesn't like it and signals a thumbs-down when Lucia isn't looking. I try not to smile. We have chocolate cake for dessert.

"Kate," asks Lucia as she pours tea from a pitcher into our cups, "what brought you to Argentina?"

I glance at Nico, who lowers his eyes. I pause before answering and wonder if I should tell her the truth: I was divorced and living in Chicago when I reconnected with a friend who asked me to live with him. He taught me how to fly-fish and escorted me to Patagonia, but I dumped him for our fishing guide. When I returned to Chicago, I cried for days missing that guide, so I left my friends and my job to be with him. The guide then dumped his girlfriend to be with me, and despite all of that, and all that's happened since, I wouldn't change a thing because that guide is Nico, and he's the love of my life.

While I ponder this I look at Nico and our eyes meet. Our relationship, though still young and tender, is strong enough to withstand any truth, but I decide to keep its intimate details private. I reach across the table and take his hand.

"It was love," I answer simply, still looking at him. "It was love."

That night we sleep well and awake the next morning to the smell of bacon. We quickly dress in our hiking clothes and grab our jackets as we head to the dining room. On the way, we pass a tall man dressed in a fleece jacket and ski pants who's standing at the front desk talking to Lucia.

"There they are," she says, walking toward us. "Kate and Nico, this is Mariano, your guide for today." I shake his hand but feel like bowing; Mariano is rumored to be the best guide for trekking the glacier. How are we so lucky?

"Hello," he says, shaking our hands. "We can leave anytime." We invite him to join us for breakfast, and the three of us head to the dining room where a buffet of meats, cheeses, cereals, and homemade breads awaits us.

"Have you ever trekked before?" Mariano asks me while eating scrambled eggs.

I look at him and smile, peeling the last of my croissant to get to its tender center. Flakes from its crust fall loosely to my plate.

"No sir," I answer, "but I walk."

He smiles at Nico, who's raising his eyebrows.

"No problem," says Mariano, "I'll take care of you."

Nico asks him about the glacier's size.

"It's about 100 square miles," he explains, "and nearly 200 feet tall at the ice wall, which is about two miles wide. The wall is at the edge of a giant lake and that's where we'll pick up the ferry."

After breakfast we head to Mariano's black Range Rover and climb inside. I sit in the passenger seat and Nico sits in back.

"Oh my God, Nico," I squeal, turning around. "We're about to trek on a glacier." He smiles while buckling his seatbelt.

"With all the walking you've been doing in San Martín," he says, "it should be easy for you. Plus, you'll be wearing crampons."

Mariano starts the Rover and nods his head.

"Sorry?" I ask. "What are those?" Nico answers.

"Spikes for your shoes, Kate, they'll grip the ice. You'll be fine."

I reach behind the seat and his hand meets mine. He squeezes it gently.

Mariano asks him something in Spanish, so I rest my head on the seat and listen while they chat in a language that I love and am only beginning to understand. I look out the window; the road is lined with poplars and pines and the bright sun appears to dance among them. Wow, a glacier, I think, closing my eyes. I begin to nap. Chicago feels like it's a universe away.

When we approach the gate to Los Glaciares National Park where Perito Moreno is located, Nico touches my shoulder to wake me. He points out the window and I gasp. The glacier is right there! I strain to look at it – its corrugated surface spans as far as I can see. It's tucked between the Andes Mountains, which are blanketed with snow, and looks otherworldly. Nothing in my life could have prepared me for it. Mariano asks if we want to stop to get a better look.

"Yes!" Nico and I answer, almost at the same time. "Let's get closer!"

A visitor's center is nearby and we park in its lot.

"You go ahead," says Mariano, pointing to a staircase. "There are balconies there. You'll be able to get much closer."

Nico and I jump from the Rover and walk briskly to the staircase, holding hands. We descend quickly to the first balcony, but want to get even closer, so continue until we get to the bottom. The glacier wall towers in front of us, and its deep, massive crevasses expose bright blue ice. I shiver with excitement, feeling privileged to see it so close.

A single tourist is taking photos and we ask him if he'll take ours. When he says yes, Nico hands him our new camera. Preparing for the photo, we stand in front of the glacier with our backs to it and quickly turn when we hear a thunderclap. We're just in time to see a giant piece of the glacier fall to the water.

"The glacier is feeding the lake," shouts Nico as he pulls me close with his arm around my waist. "We're lucky to see this together!" He kisses me while the tourist finally takes our photo.

After we leave the visitor's center, we head to the ferry that will take us to our trek. The parking lot is full of cars and as we walk along the plank to climb aboard, I hear people talking in various languages. I recognize Spanish, French, German, and Italian.

"A melting pot," I inform Nico as we take our places near the front of the boat. He nods his head. As the ferry crawls slowly to the other end of the lake, we watch as the glacier's wall gets closer and closer. The air, which up to now has been warm, begins to get cooler as we approach the ice.

When we reach the dock, we disembark and hike along a long dirt trail surrounded by pine trees. The trail will lead us to huts where guides will attach crampons to our hiking shoes.

"Make sure that your shoes are on tight," warns Mariano as he walks beside us, "otherwise the crampons, which are very heavy, will pull your shoes off when you're walking up the glacier."

At the huts, Nico and I climb onto a bench where guides, sitting at our feet like shoe shiners, tie on the crampons, which are nothing more than heavy metal platforms attached to thick metal spikes. The platforms are secured with yards of black ribbon-like cloth. While my guide is wrapping my feet, I look at the glacier, which is at least a mile away. Squinting against the sun, I see what appear to be deer climbing up a steep snowy trail. Nico turns to see where I'm looking.

"Those are trekkers, Kate," he says, smiling. "That's where we're going." His guide turns to look.

"*Sí, senorita*," he says, "*es un largo viaje* (Yes, miss, it is a long journey)."

The crampons are heavy and we're told to wear gloves in case we fall on the ice. As Nico and I begin our trek, he takes my hand.

"You OK with this?" he asks. "We can turn back if you don't want to do it."

I smile and slip my arm around his waist.

"I'm OK if you're OK," I tell him.

The glacier's surface is mushy and our metal spikes easily grip the ice. Nico walks behind me.

"I'll catch you if you fall," he explains.

Our group includes all ages and nationalities and we trek together, single-file. Despite our differences, right now we're a team. The sky is clear and the sun's reflection off the glacier is so bright that we all wear sunglasses to protect our eyes from the glare.

"With your crampons, sunglasses and gloves, you all look like you're from a different planet," shouts Mariano, who treks back and forth next to the line to ensure we're safe.

The area that we trek is minute compared to the glacier's massive size. Along the way, we pass deep crevasses and pools of water created by melted snow. The water looks blue. At one point, the heel of my shoe slips off and Nico secures it. The trek is surprisingly easy, thanks to the crampons and my months of walking in San Martín.

After an hour the trek is over, and we toast our journey with whiskey at a small refreshment station.

"You made it!" announces Mariano. "Now it's time to celebrate!" And as a group, we toast.

On the way down, Nico walks in front of me again to guard me from falling. When we return to the ferry after a short lunch, he slaps Mariano on the back.

"What do you think of my girl on that glacier?" he asks. I blush and smile.

We have dinner that night with Lucia and Jorge and tell them about our trek. I'm sitting next to Nico and during dessert he puts his hand on my knee, looks at me and grins.

"We should get a good night's sleep because we're trekking to the lagoon at the base of Mt. Fitz Roy day after tomorrow," he says. "Fitz Roy is the mountain range that inspired the Patagonia clothing label."

Lucia looks at Jorge and smiles.

"We did that last year," she says. "It's not an easy trek. Who's your guide?"

I look at Nico without smiling; I've read about Fitz Roy. Its elevation is about 12,000 feet and the lagoon is just a few thousand less than that. The trail is very steep.

"Pablo is our guide," replies Nico, turning to Lucia. "He's a friend of Mariano's. He's supposed to be the best guide in

Argentina."

I'm staring at Nico and don't know what to say. I nudge him under the table.

"I'm sorry, Kate," he says, looking at me. "I should have told you, but I thought you would be happy about it. It's supposed to be one of the most beautiful treks on earth."

I look at Lucia and Jorge and they're staring at us. I sit up straight in the chair.

"OK," I say reluctantly. "I'm game."

When we get back to our room I tell Nico how I really feel.

"I'm worried," I say, "I've read that the Fitz Roy trek is at least seven hours to get to the lagoon from town. I don't know if I can handle that. And I don't want to let you down."

Nico pulls me onto the bed and takes my hands in his.

"It will be OK," he says in a soothing tone. "I will take care of you. Pablo can trek in front and I'll trek in back. We'll be like bookends. Nothing will happen. This trek will help you to learn to trust me." I stare at him before I speak.

"I trust you, Nico. You don't think I do?" He squeezes my hands.

"I know that it's been difficult dealing with me and Marina. I'm sure you wonder about us. But that's over. I love you."

THE NEXT MORNING we start our four-hour drive to El Chaltén, a small mountain village known as Argentina's trekking capital. Nico explains as we drive that "chaltén" means "smoking mountain."

"It's because the Tehuelches thought the clouds circling Fitz Roy looked like smoke," he adds.

"The what?" I ask, scanning the countryside looking for animals.

"T-e-h-u-e-l-c-h-e," he responds, "it means fierce people, and they were the native tribes of Patagonia. Are you paying attention to me?"

I start to answer but tell him to pull over when I see a flock of pink birds drinking from a distant pond. He follows my gaze.

"Flamingos!" he exclaims. "Now that's something you don't see in San Martín."

We pull to the side of the road so that I can take a photograph, and I stride briskly into the field. When a wire fence blocks my passage, I shoot the photo from this distance. I return to the car and show the photo to Nico. All we can see are tiny pink dots.

"No one will know what they are," I complain.

"It's OK," he says, beginning to drive, "we will know."

An hour later, Nico suddenly pulls to the shoulder of the road. He points to a condor that's swooping down in front of us, nearly hitting a nearby road sign before it flies up toward the mountains. I recognize what it is by its white collar.

"Wow," he says. "You never see that! Condors live in the mountains and they like to hide."

As I watch the condor fly away, I see Fitz Roy in the distance. From here it looks like a poorly crafted arrowhead. It's the tallest mountain in the range, which is covered with snow, and since it's overcast, from here the entire range looks almost ghostly, as if it doesn't exist at all.

"Incredible, isn't it?" asks Nico, watching me. "It's made of granite. It's among the most challenging peaks in the world to climb. Only a few people have successfully reached its summit. We're just climbing to its base."

I watch Fitz Roy get closer while we drive. We're the only travelers on this two-lane road, which is newly paved and stretches for miles through a vast hilly steppe. We ride in silence as I take photos of farmhouses and horses with our new camera. I take several photos of Nico until he pushes the camera away.

"Enough!" he says. I can tell he's annoyed, and I set the camera in my lap. I decide to press him.

"Don't you realize how handsome you are?"

He shakes his head. I look at him in disbelief and it suddenly occurs to me that I've never told him how I felt when I first saw him, how I longed for him and couldn't stand the thought of never seeing him again.

"Nico, please pull over for a second, I want to say something to you but I don't want to distract you while you're driving."

"OK," he says, hesitantly. "You haven't changed your mind about this trip, have you?"

"No!" I exclaim after he stops the car. "Remember when we first met?"

He nods his head and turns to me. I continue.

"I thought I had died and gone to heaven. I had never felt such intense attraction. It was immediate, intense and it hasn't gone away. Instead, the feelings have just grown stronger. I'm sorry to say this for Clay and Andrew, who are good men. But I can't think of anyone I'd rather be with than you. If you decide to return to Marina, I would understand. More than anything, I want you to be happy."

"And," I continue, jokingly, "I want you to know all of this now in case when we're trekking Fitz Roy, I fall off and die."

He smiles at me and I can see that he's blushing. I know he doesn't like this much attention and doesn't think of himself as handsome. Instead, he thinks of himself as a fly-fisherman who is strong, capable, smart, and skilled in one of the most difficult sports to master.

"Thank you, Kate," he says, shifting the car back into drive. "We should probably get to the hotel."

I lean back in my seat and smile. Now it's clear to him. Importantly, it's clear to me, too.

We arrive in El Chaltén in the late afternoon and find our hotel, which has only two stories and is of contemporary design. It has a double front door made of solid wood and the door handles are giant metal rings.

Nico sets our luggage at the front desk and after checking in, we go to our room, which is on the second floor. The room is beautiful. It has large windows, bright red walls, a desk, and a queen-sized bed with a contemporary print hanging at its head.

The hotel doesn't serve dinner, so after unpacking we head to the lobby to inquire about restaurants. A man wearing hiking clothes and a backpack enters the hotel, smiles at us and extends his hand. His eyes are bright and his smile is wide. He exudes friendliness.

"*¡Hola!*" he says cheerfully as he walks over. "I'm Pablo. Are you Nico and Kate?" He sets his backpack on the floor to shake our hands.

Any fear that I had about trekking Fitz Roy dissipates in that moment. Pablo appears confident, strong and capable. He's also endearing.

"Let's sit in the lobby for a few minutes so that we can talk," he says, grabbing a thick packet of papers from his backpack. "I brought maps to show you where we're going tomorrow."

He spreads the maps on a coffee table and we gather around to look. The maps are topographical and show incredible detail. Pablo excitedly tells us where we're headed.

"We'll start at a low grade for a few hours," he explains, "until we begin to reach the actual trail to Fitz Roy. It's not an easy trek. Are you sure you want to do it?"

Nico looks at me and I nod.

"Looks like she's willing," he says to Pablo. "Now, where can we go for dinner?"

CHAPTER 17
PLAY

Early the next morning we meet Pablo in front of the hotel. The sky is clear but the temperature is cool, so Nico and I each wear hiking pants, a T-shirt, fleece jacket, and hiking boots with thick wool socks. We've brought our backpacks, which contain plastic water bottles, suntan lotion, bug spray, and Band-Aids.

When we see Pablo, he's chatting with a woman who has curly brown hair. She's petite and beautiful; he introduces her as Marijke, his girlfriend.

"Hello!" she says, cheerfully, hugging us. "I'm going to drive you to the mountain and will pick you up later."

We decide to drive our rental car, so Marijke and Pablo climb in the backseat and he drapes an arm around her shoulders.

"How do you like Patagonia so far?" Marijke asks me, leaning forward.

I look at Nico but since he's concentrating on driving, he doesn't answer.

"It's wonderful!" I answer.

We chat for a few minutes and I learn that she's Dutch, teaches yoga in the mountains and prepares the food for Pablo's treks. For most of our drive, she and Pablo speak to each other in Spanish.

She, too, I think, has come from a foreign country to be with the one she loves. And like me, she cares enough to learn his language.

We drive for nearly 30 minutes along a rutted dirt road. When we reach the trailhead, Marijke takes a photo of me, Nico and Pablo.

"This photo is before your trek," she says, teasing us, "and I'll take another one after you get back so you can see how much weight you've lost."

As she drives off, dust swirling at the back of the car, we pull on our backpacks. Pablo's backpack is twice the size of ours and he explains that it's because it contains our lunches and a first aid kit.

As we begin to walk, I scan the horizon for Fitz Roy and soon see its peak through the tree line. It appears surprisingly close. Lit by the sun, its granite surface seems to shine and it's powdered with snow.

Feeling challenged, but strong, I clip my backpack strap across my chest and pull it tight.

"Let's do this!" I declare.

Our trek begins on flat land and is easy at first, so we walk slowly to enjoy the surrounding vegetation. We see bushes with tiny red flowers, trees of various species and a variety of grasses, tall and short. We walk without speaking until Pablo asks Nico about fishing.

"How long have you been doing it?" he asks.

"Since I was very young," answers Nico. "My older brother taught me."

For a few minutes they chat in Spanish, and I understand enough to realize they're talking about San Martín. And then I hear Nico say my name.

"Kate *y yo vivimos fuera de la ciudad* (Kate and I live out of town)." Watching him, I feel the familiar tingling of attraction as he continues to speak in Spanish, and I wonder what he's saying. When Pablo turns to smile at me, I hear Nico say, *"Sí, ella es maravillosa* (Yes, she's very brave)."

Our trek gets more difficult as we get closer to Fitz Roy since our trail is getting steep. I'm warmer, so I take off my fleece jacket and tuck it into my backpack. The terrain changes as we approach several giant boulders.

"Let's stop here," says Pablo, dropping his backpack on the ground. He leads us a few feet down the trail and points. Directly in front of us is a mountain that looks split in two. On top is a snowy glacier cascading from its crest. The glacier ends at a frozen lake.

Nico and I wrap our arms around each other's waists and stare.

"Those glaciers are not to be stopped," he says, kissing my head. "They're sort of like you."

We continue to trek for nearly five hours before reaching the bottom of the trail that leads to Fitz Roy. Before we ascend, we stop at a narrow stream to fill our water bottles and eat half our lunch, which includes miniature quiches, whole-grain muffins, nuts, and apples. There are large rocks everywhere, scattered as if by an avalanche, and a narrow wooden bridge for crossing the stream.

As we sit next to the stream and eat, we watch a man and woman descend from the Fitz Roy trail with a young girl strapped in a covered harness on the man's back. When the couple walks past us we wave, and they wave back. I smile when the girl's tiny hand emerges and she waves, too.

"It's good to know that the trail is easy enough to take a child," I suggest to Pablo, who's drinking from his water bottle. "How hard can it be?"

He smiles and tightens the bottle's cap.

"They probably only went halfway," he replies. "It gets steeper as you get higher. The last hour is nearly straight up." He demonstrates with his hand; his fingers point to the sky. He directs my attention to the trail. High above us, it looks like a tiny scar on the mountain with just a few switchbacks in a field of grass.

"It looks easy," says Pablo as he stands up. "But it's not."

Nico grabs my backpack from the ground and stuffs it into his.

"Don't worry, Kate," he says, "I'll walk behind you. Nothing will happen. You're strong enough."

I only felt strong once, and it was the last time my mother tried to attack me. I was sleeping on the living room couch after school.

When she returned home from work, she woke me by shaking my legs.

"Kate, get up," she demanded. "Do you have homework?"

I smelled alcohol on her breath and sat up.

"You're drunk," I mouthed. She lunged at me, but instead of running, I grabbed her wrists.

"No!" I cried as she started screaming. I gripped her tight, but she pulled away. I ran to my bedroom, slammed the door and locked it. She never attacked me again.

The trail to Fitz Roy appears to be man-made. Carved into the mountain and supplemented with boulders, it's fashioned like a simple staircase, yet each rise is at least two feet high. We walk for two hours before reaching its midpoint when we stop. Nearly breathless, I call out to Pablo.

"I…can't…do…this," I pant. "I'm…afraid…I'll knock…Nico off the mountain."

Pablo rushes to stand behind me.

"Kate, we're almost there," he coaxes, as Nico rests his hand on my shoulder. "It's just a few more steps."

Thirty minutes later we reach level ground, and I scan the horizon. It's beautiful, with massive lakes and rolling hills. I bend over to stretch my hamstrings and Nico stands beside me.

"You're here!" shouts Pablo, proudly walking around with his arms outstretched. "Isn't it beautiful?" I stand and look around to find the lagoon, but it isn't there. I see that the trail hasn't ended. Pablo wants to give me an out. I take a deep breath before speaking.

"We're not there," I tell him, "we should keep going."

Pablo raises his eyebrows and looks at Nico, who nods his head.

"OK," he says, handing me my water bottle. "But you should drink so you don't get dehydrated."

Minutes later while climbing, I slip, and Nico gently lays his hand on my back to steady me. His touch feels reassuring and I turn to look at him. He long ago removed his fleece jacket and tied it to his waist, and his sunglasses are perched on his head. The skin on his face and arms is moist from sweating and his T-shirt, once white, shows dirt where he's wiped his hands. He's carrying my backpack as well as his, yet despite this extra load, he smiles at me. Even now, after hours of heavy trekking and just yards away from Fitz Roy, one of the most spectacular mountains on earth, I can't keep my eyes off him. After a few seconds, I hear Pablo call my name.

"Kate! You OK?" Reluctantly, I turn and nod while I continue to climb.

When we finally reach our destination, we cheer. Fitz Roy is still about a mile away; between the mountain and us are a small glacier, ridgeline and frozen lake covered with snow. Pablo points to a few trekkers who reached the top of the ridgeline and are skiing down.

"Extreme sports," he laughs.

Nico stands behind me, wraps his arms around my chest and presses his cheek against mine. I relax my body into his.

"It's magic, isn't it?" he whispers. "Magic."

Eager to get back to town before dark, we quickly trek down the trail and fill our water bottles when we reach the stream. It's at least three more hours until we get back to our hotel and my feet are already hurting. About 20 minutes later, we pass an old log house and Pablo tells us he's going behind it to "take care of some business."

When he does, Nico and I sit on a bench near the front door and he takes my hand. There's no wind and the area is quiet, except for a singing bird.

"Kate," he says, "we have a few minutes and I want to say something." I squeeze his fingers and he continues.

"Remember when you asked me in the restaurant why I'm with you? Well, before I met you, I felt a bit lost." He pauses and shuffles his feet along the ground. The movement stirs up a small cloud of dust and he brushes it away.

"I mean, I love to fish and guide and I'm good at it, but Marina didn't like that, and I wanted to please her, to take care of her, you know, because of her arm." He pauses again before continuing and rubs his hand through his hair.

"Men here do that, you know, provide for their families. I knew Marina so long she was like family to me and I felt committed to her, like her protector, but she never seemed happy. It was never enough. She wanted me to stop guiding and to take care of her. She loved me for what I could give her and not for who I am."

He pauses for a moment and his mouth tightens as if he tastes something unpleasant.

"Then," he says, "I met you, and you didn't need to be taken care of. You're beautiful, smart and strong, you fish and you ride and now I see that you can trek." He smiles at me before continuing.

"But," he adds, "those aren't the only reasons I love you. I love you because you're kind and giving, and you care about me."

I stare at him, surprised. How could anyone *not* care about this strong and wonderful man? Moving closer, he wraps his arm around my shoulders.

"I love the way you accept me for who I am and you never ask me to change. You support my choices, and you forgive my weaknesses. And when you look at me, it's like I'm the only person on the planet. You respect my desire to live here and you want me to be happy. I know that you truly love me, Kate. I feel it every single day."

I hear Pablo walking through the grass so I quickly stand, take Nico's hand and pull him close.

"I do love you," I whisper in his ear as he wraps his arms around me. "I love you every single day."

THE NEXT MORNING we have breakfast in the lobby and leave

around 8. We pack our bags into the car, drive to Calafate and turn in our car. Nico hands me my boarding pass, we board the plane and find our seats. As I'm buckling my seatbelt, he leans over and smiles at me.

"One last treat," he says, his eyes shining. I look at him, surprised. He takes my hand and places my palm on his cheek. His beard, like his hair, is soft and silky. "Want to see the whales?"

At first I don't understand, then remember that a major attraction in Patagonia is whale watching off the Valdés Peninsula on Argentina's east coast.

I open my eyes wide. "Now?" I ask, surprised.

"Yes," he answers. "Now."

I once told Nico that I didn't get to play very much when I was growing up.

"Too much responsibility," I said one night while we were eating dinner, "at too young an age." He nodded and I thought he wasn't paying much attention.

Later that night as we lay together on the living room couch reading the local newspaper, I realized I was wrong.

"I'm sorry your dad died when you were so young, Kate. We'll have to figure out a way for you to play. Not so much responsibility."

I never told him that my mother hit me. I didn't want him to feel my pain.

Our plane lands at Trelew Airport, which is about 39 miles from Puerto Madryn, a seaside village where we'll be staying before our excursion. It's just a few hours from the peninsula. At the airport we rent a car and drive to our hotel where we buy tickets for our whale-watching excursion. We're scheduled to leave the next morning to see the whales, which at this time of year are still with their calves. We're also scheduled to see elephant seals and Magellanic penguins that live on the coast. I've read that Magellanic penguins were named after Ferdinand Magellan, who first spotted them in the early 16th century.

Our room overlooks the water and has a patio; Nico opens the doors to let in the fresh air.

"I went to Bolivia so that I could take us on this trip," he says, walking over to me. "I'm telling you so that you know I wasn't just abandoning you. I wanted to take you somewhere to play."

I look at him for several seconds. I can't speak.

"You and I are family now," he continues, wrapping his arms around me. "I know I'm not as good as your real family, but I am family just the same."

I begin to cry and he holds me closer. This time I cry because I'm overwhelmed by happiness; how am I so lucky to be with this wonderful man? I look at him and struggle for something to say.

"*Nunca he sentido amor como este* (I've never felt love like this)," I finally whisper. "*Es el mejor tipo de amor* (It is the best kind of love).” And then I kiss him, tenderly, on the cheek.

That night we eat pizza and drink beer at a pub next to the hotel, and when we return to our hotel we fall asleep early, still exhausted from our Fitz Roy trek.

In the morning we eat breakfast in the hotel dining room, and at 9 a.m. our excursion van picks us up near the front door. Two other couples are already in the van: a man and woman from Spain and two men from Germany. Nico and I climb in the rear seat and the guide, Tamara, sits in front, next to the driver. She’s wearing sunglasses with large round lenses and large silver hoop earrings with a tiny black bead hanging from each one. Her dark hair is clipped with a large tortoiseshell comb. As we drive onto the road, she tells us about the whales.

“They’re called southern right whales here,” she explains, “but you may know them as baleen whales elsewhere.”

Nico and I hold hands while Tamara explains to us that the ocean might be too choppy for us to see the whales today. We look at each other, disappointed.

“But you’ll still see the penguins for sure, so we’ll go there first,” she says. “There are thousands of them on the beach now.”

Nico leans over and gently pulls my ponytail, which is wrapped with a red scrunchie.

“Told you we would play,” he whispers in my ear.

Grateful, I squeeze his knee and kiss him on the cheek.

“And I can’t think of anyone I’d rather play with,” I whisper back. “We’ll have a whale of a time.” Laughing, he hugs me tight.

When we arrive at the peninsula, the driver parks near a small information center and we all go inside to learn about the area's wildlife. After touring the exhibits, we leave the center through a back door that leads to a balcony on the beach, and immediately see several large animals sunning themselves on the sand. From here they look like giant sausage links.

"Elephant seals," explains Tamara. "Watch the water."

We turn our attention to the shoreline and see nothing but rocks. Suddenly, one of the rocks moves and emerges from the water, and we realize that it's an elephant seal. It's small and Tamara says it's a cub. We watch as it shimmies onto the beach as if running.

Within moments, another seal leaves the water, and this time it's much larger.

"Must be its mother," says Tamara. The mother seal shimmies quickly after the cub until it stops several yards from the water. The mother scoots beside it, stops and lays a fin on the cub's back. She snuggles close.

"Awww," we all say in unison as we clap our hands. I say to Nico, "She's protecting it," and he nods.

We leave the balcony to walk along a sandy trail that's delineated by shells and rocks.

"It's a border to protect the penguin nests," explains Tamara.

Curious, we look for the nests and find them. Each is a large hole in the sand about two feet deep. Most of the nests are empty, but one has a penguin curled up inside. The penguin appears to be sleeping, but lazily opens its eyes when we get near. Otherwise, it doesn't move.

I'm surprised at how small the penguins are. They barely reach my knees. Yet, they're quite bold. One stands in the middle of the trail with its eyes closed as two eggs poke out of its brood pouch. Another stands nearby with its beak pointed at the sky as if relishing the warm sun. It seems to be smiling.

When we reach the end of the trail, Nico takes my hand and leads me toward an open concrete bench. Beneath is a penguin and it looks as if it's hiding. As we walk by, it peers out.

"It's considering an exit strategy," I say to Nico, who is laughing and taking photos.

After we get back into the van, we head for the ocean.

"We can see the whales after all," Tamara announces. "The ocean has gotten calmer. We'll be there soon."

We drive for several miles; Nico lays his head on my shoulder and naps while I read a pamphlet about the whales. When we arrive at the dock, the boat captain instructs us that we need to wear life vests. We board, put on our sunglasses and sit on a bench next to the boat's railing. Like on the glacier ferry, the boat is packed with international tourists, including several from England. We try to chat with them as we head out to sea, but the boat engine is too loud. Since the waves are high and the ride is rough, Nico and I hold onto the railing. When the seawater splashes on us, Nico cleans the lenses of my sunglasses with his little finger so that I can see. After a few minutes, we hear Tamara's voice.

"Port!" she cries, and we look to our left. Yards away there's a breaching whale, and next to it is another, but smaller.

"A calf!" shouts Nico, as he grabs the camera from his jacket pocket. For the next few minutes, we watch as the whale and its calf swim, dive and breach alongside the boat. We're surprised to see several seagulls flying around the whales, so I ask Tamara about them.

"The seagulls like to attack the whales for their skin and blubber!" she responds.

But I watch as one seagull, seemingly unfazed by the breaching and splashing, simply floats behind the whales. The force of the active water pulls it forward, so I yell to Nico that it's their chaperone. He turns to me, wipes mist off his sunglasses with his sleeve and smiles.

At the end of the day, the van drops us off at our hotel. It's dinnertime but we're too tired to eat. Instead, we collapse on our bed with our clothes on and sleep until midnight. When we awaken, Nico turns his head on the pillow to look at me.

"What do you think?" he asks, smoothing the hair from my face. "Did we play enough?"

I smile, nod and kiss him.

"Yes," I respond, pulling my shirt over my head. "Except we have one more activity before we leave tomorrow, and we can do that without leaving this room."

CHAPTER 18
MARRY

On November 1, Nico suggests that we fish together on the Chimehuin River. It's the first day of the new season.

"We can fish together for old time's sake," he explains.

When we get to the white house, he tells me he wants to air it out since it has been closed for the winter.

"I'll just open a few windows," he says. "It won't take long."

When we step into the living room, I am surprised to see fresh lilacs everywhere – in vases, baskets and carefully scattered on the floor. The furniture has been pushed back against the wall, and a small table with two chairs is set in the middle for lunch.

In the center of the table there is a single bowl of large green olives.

Nico looks at me and smiles.

"Ah-love olives," he says. "Right?"

I look at him, throw my arms around his neck and kiss him.

"Yes!" I exclaim. "You remembered!"

Then he takes my hand, kneels and pulls a white box from his pocket.

"Will you please marry me, Kate?" he asks, opening the box.

Tucked inside is a diamond ring surrounded by tiny fishing flies. The largest one is an inchworm. I know that he tied it himself.

Cupping his face in my hands, I kneel down beside him.

"Yes," I respond, kissing him. "*No quiero nada más en el mundo* (There's nothing more I want in the world)."

WHEN I CALLED EVA she was ecstatic and apologized for doubting Nico. Then she and Jason flew to Patagonia so we could celebrate. They brought Gus.

"Holy shit," he said when I picked them up at the airport. "It's the end of the world here. Now, where's Nico?"

When they met, Nico jokingly told Gus that I was fully Argentine now and that he had to leave me alone.

"You mean she's not coming back with me to Chicago?" Gus joked. Nico shook his head.

Nico's parents, wanting to meet my friends, arranged an *asado* on the Chimehuin River near the white house. In addition to my U.S. friends, others came, too: Mike, Rubén and all of Nico's guide friends, as well as Nidra, Fede and Diego.

"I hear you like to feed deer," said Gus to Diego while they sat together at the picnic table munching on chorizo.

"*¿Dónde más van a comer?* (Where else will they eat)," Diego replied, then in English added, "this place is so damned dry."

Gus, wrinkling his brow trying to figure out the Spanish, finally just agreed, and the two of them sealed their new friendship with a fist bump.

As the evening ended, Eva and I walked to the river and sat on a downed willow tree next to the water.

"Wow, Katie," she said. "Who knew?"

I smiled and hooked my arm through hers. We were silent for a few seconds before she spoke again.

"What is it about Nico that you didn't have with Clay or Andrew?" I thought for a moment before answering.

"It's love, Eva. It started with sexual attraction but it grew to be something more." I paused.

She looked at me and smiled, indicating that I should continue.

"I don't think I knew what love was until I met Nico," I said. "There was always an agenda before – with Clay it was figuring out our careers, and with Andrew it was submitting to his dominance. He always needed to be in control and he always kept score."

Eva nodded her head in agreement.

"Nico and I don't have a spreadsheet relationship," I continued. "Our love is real."

I leaned over, picked up a rock, rubbed it on my sleeve, and handed it to her.

"Nico taught me that when you love someone, you try not to hurt them," I said.

I wrapped my arms around my knees as Nico quietly walked up behind us. He leaned gently against my back and stroked my hair. I looked up at him and smiled.

"*Nunca he sentido amor como este,*" I said. "*Es el mejor tipo de amor.*" Then I looked at Eva.

"I'm learning that real love is kind, and is as solid as that rock that you hold in your hand."

I stood, walked to Nico and took his hand. We both looked at the Chimehuin, its glassy surface shining in the moonlight. I thought I saw a fish rise and nudged him, and he nudged back.

Smiling, he helped Eva to her feet.

"Let's go ladies," he said. "We can fish tomorrow."

Then carefully leading us through the underbrush, he guided us back to the *asado* to celebrate with our family and friends.

Acknowledgments

The author wishes to thank the following individuals who helped her to complete this book:

MARY ELLEN BENSON (EDITOR)

Mary Ellen Benson is a writer and editor who lives in St. Louis, Mo. She has a degree in English from Vassar College. In some ways, she never left college — in addition to writing and teaching, she spent much of her career in higher education administration, principally at Washington University in St. Louis. An avid bicyclist, her favorite escape is being on the bike trails with her husband, Willy Thierheimer, or dining out with friends.

AVA EHRLICH (REVIEWER)

Ava Ehrlich is a senior broadcast manager at KSDK-TV in St. Louis. A broadcast veteran, she has worked in several markets. She has Bachelor of Science in Journalism and Master of Science in Journalism degrees from the Medill School of Journalism at Northwestern University, as well as a Master of Arts in Urban Affairs from Occidental College in Los Angeles. A lifelong college instructor, she has spent the last 20 years as an adjunct faculty member at Washington University in St. Louis. Ava loves reading, working out (though no athlete), movies, plays, and mahjong. With her husband Barry Freedman, her main interest is keeping track of her two adult sons. It's harder with the second, a consultant in Chicago. However, her first-born is an AAA baseball announcer, so she spends the season listening to at least part of all 140 games.

KATIE STIEHL FRAUENFELDER (REVIEWER)

Katie Frauenfelder is a personal trainer and nutritionist residing in St. Louis, Mo. She graduated from Bradley University with a bachelor's degree in dietetics and is currently pursuing a master's degree in counseling from Lindenwood University. She loves hanging out with her family and friends, lives to travel and is passionate about fitness.

MARCY MAMROTH (DESIGNER)

Marcy Mamroth is a freelance graphic designer who lives in St. Louis, Mo. She grew up in Highland Park, Ill., and later lived in Lincoln Park in Chicago. She has a Bachelor of Arts degree from Sophie Newcomb College/Tulane University. A large part of her career was spent at Levy Restaurants in Chicago as Creative Director. Marcy moved to St. Louis when she married her husband Merritt. She loves using her creativity in different mediums, enjoys reading and loves being with family and friends.

GEORG MICIU (COVER ARTIST)

Georg Miciu was born in Austria, and at the age of 3 years moved with his parents to Argentina since his family wanted to escape the war in Europe. As a young man, he studied the great masters of art in the United States, South America, Canada, Mexico, Europe, and the Middle East, all the while perfecting the *"en plein air"* (painting outdoors) technique. During this period, he adopted the palette knife as his primary painting tool (depicted on the cover). Georg's paintings of the Patagonia landscape and culture are legendary and have been exhibited in more than 300 venues, including the South American cities of Rosario, Córdoba, Buenos Aires, Bariloche, and Mar del Plata as well as Granada and Almeria in Spain, and the U.S. cities of San Francisco, Montecito, and Palm Beach. In 2005, he opened the beautiful "Colección Georg" art gallery near his home in San Martín de los Andes where his numerous paintings are displayed along with the works of his nine artistically talented children.

CHRISTINA STIEHL (REVIEWER)

Christina Stiehl is a writer and editor living in New York City. She grew up near St. Louis, and after graduating from the University of Missouri School of Journalism with a bachelor's degree in magazine journalism, moved to New York to pursue her dream of being a professional writer. By day, she works as the Editor for the party planning and lifestyle publication Celebrations.com. By night, she pretends to be a mixologist and DIYer, and blogs about it on SassintheCityBlog.com

In addition, the author wishes to thank the staff at LOL Argentina Tourism Solutions and Chocolate Lab Expeditions as well as the many talented, hardworking, kind, patient, and generous Argentina guides who introduced her to the vast and beautiful Patagonia landscape. Visit revealpatagonia.com to see it for yourself.